A Small Town in Africa

Daisy Waugh is a freelance journalist, writing
regularly for the *Evening Standard*, *Spectator* and other
national newspapers and magazines. She has written
one novel, *What is the matter with Mary Jane?* She lives
in London.

A
Small
Town
in Africa

DAISY WAUGH

Mandarin

A Mandarin Paperback
A SMALL TOWN IN AFRICA

First published in Great Britain 1994
by William Heinemann Ltd
This edition published 1995
by Mandarin Paperbacks
an imprint of Reed Books Ltd
Michelin House, 81 Fulham Road, London SW3 6RB
and Auckland, Melbourne, Singapore and Toronto

Reprinted 1995

A CIP catalogue record for this title
is available from the British Library
ISBN 0 7493 1670 5

Printed and bound in Great Britain by
BPC Paperbacks Ltd
A member of
The British Printing Company Ltd

For my parents, with love

Acknowledgements

Alexander and Eliza, I don't think I can ever thank you enough.

Thank you Selina and Amaury Blow, Royal Bank of Scotland, Taunton Branch, Miles Bredin, Jeremy Swift and Ivo Philipps.

Cast

Bill	American Peace Corps volunteer. My landlord for a few months. Catholic.
Mr and Mrs Sweet	English couple. Mr Sweet has many degrees. Works on an aid project for the British Government in Isiolo. C of E.
Hassan	Young, well-dressed Somali bangle boy. About nineteen. Lives well. Good friend. Moslem.
Achmed and Fauzia	Bill's and my neighbours. Have many children. Television set. Friends. Arab Moslems.
Maria, Hassan (Junior), Hussein, Salma	Some of their children. Moslem.
Mr Job	Electrician. Jewellery maker. Wears western clothes in Isiolo, Samburu clothes in Samburu. Good friend. No specific religion.
Nassir	Somali businessman. Late twenties. One of thirty relatively prosperous brothers, many of whom live in town. Seems to give most of his money to waifs. Good friend. Moslem.
Zulecha and Maria	Teenage schoolgirls. Cousins/sisters. Rarely seen apart. Boran tribe. Moslem.

Zaidi	Maria's sister and guardian. Rich, laid back, lazy, beautiful. Mother of several. Boran. Moslem.
Professor	Somali poet in exile. Broke. Warm, wise, clever, funny. Sick. Good friend. Communist.
Wanjella	Ugly lips. Broken dreams. A sad man. Christian.
Kabede	Ethiopian physician/shoe vendor. Father of four. Television set. Ambitious. Low church Christian.
Esther, Janet, Moulu, Grace	His children. My pupils.
Seileesh	Indian. Best friend of Bill's. Rich. Wears jewellery. Smokes Benson and Hedges. Rarely does any work. Mid thirties. Apparently without religion.
Mama Fatima	Maria's mother. Ugly, clever, frightening. Sits on councils. Lives alone with several children. Boran. Moslem.
Issac	Works at the bank. Close friend of Nassir's. Serious. Political. Friend. Moslem.
Miss Kathurima	First headmistress. Incompetent. Humorous. Lazy. Engaged to be married. Meru tribe. Christian.
Mrs Tacho	Tall headmistress. Indian. Married to Boranni (very rare). Serious. Quite frightening. Moslem.
John and Chris	American tourists with lots of money. Something to do with Bill
Douglas	American tourist with no money. Something to do with Lamu.
Peter	Bangle boy. Laid back, slightly crooked, humorous. About nineteen. Well dressed.

	Tribe not known. Religion apparently not important.
Japan	Ageing bangle boy. Not up to much good. Boran tribe. Religion clearly not important.
Ali	Scoundrel. Bangle boy. Crook.
Lucy	Ambitious post office girl. Married with children but lives alone.
Monica	Lies under the fruit-selling tree and asks for presents. Always laughs. Often gives something in return.
Nancy	Could be Monica's daughter, could not. Also lies under the fruit-selling tree. Fat. Speaks English like a Shakespearean actress. Can't cook mandazi. Fairly irritating.
Mary	Mother of Kelvin. Lies under the fruit-selling tree. Friend.
Swahili Teacher	Astoundingly irritating older man. Loves to talk. Takes himself very seriously. Polite. Well-meaning. Bit of a bore. Luo tribe. Christian.
The Gigalos	Silly boys with too much money and not enough to do. One of them is a nephew of Nassir's. Somalis. Moslems.
The Crooked Watchman	Brigand.
Golden Finger	Somali brigand. Tramp. Brilliant dancer. Very funny.
Bernard	Neat manager of my lodge. Borrows money to buy spot cream. Meru tribe. Christian.
Mohammed	Madman with Land Rover for hire. Christian/Moslem/Christian/Moslem.

A Few Words

Mzungu	White (person)
Wazungu	White people
Miraa	A twig from which the bark is pulled off and chewed for a speed-like high
Habari?	How are you?
Habari safari/chakula?	How was the journey/food?
Mzuri	Good
Mzuri sana	Very good
Acuna matata	It doesn't matter
Mwalimu	Teacher
Matatu	(Overcrowded) minibus
Salama	Peaceful
Harambe	Collection (from a group, of money)
Ugali	Tasteless, white, glue-like food; staple diet for many
Choo	Lavatory
Nipé	Give me
Giko	Small stove, runs on wood
Mandazi	Deep fried bread/doughnut without jam or sugar
Hapana	No
Kuja!	Come!
We!	You!
Panga	Big Kenyan knife
Matatu	Overcrowded, badly driven minibus. Many hundreds die on them each year

All spellings of people's names have been derived phonetically
1 Kenyan shilling (ksh) = 2p at the time of writing

PART ONE

The ex-pats in Nairobi are horrified by my plans. They titter when they see how ignorant I am. They tell me about the troops of killer ants which march over bedclothes in the bush. They tell me about the little insects which travel through your piss, eat up your belly from the inside to the out; about the other ones that come in through the soles of your feet and make nests for themselves in your brain.

'Well,' says an English man one morning (my first morning) when I am quite sick, quite skinny with nerves, 'clearly you haven't prepared. You'll deserve whatever you get . . . Have they given us the marmalade?'

I have been wanting to come to East Africa for nearly fifteen years – ever since my primary school headmistress came back from Uganda, I think it was, and showed us her holiday slides. So here I am, with twenty-three years of elegant living behind me and a troop of killer ants ahead. I think I have fixed myself up with a job as a teacher in a small town some way beyond Mount Kenya. I have read the paragraph about Isiolo in my travel book, and a friend of mine claims to have driven through it once. I asked him what it was like but he wasn't too clear. 'Well,' he said,

'it's just like a typical African town, you know, really.'
Did they have electricity, then? He couldn't remember.
Running water? Er– It isn't surprising, I suppose, that
the ex-pats titter. But it doesn't help.

*

My breakfast host has put me in contact with a kinder
expat called Mr O'Rourke. Although he's been living in
Isiolo (building a hospital) for the past three years, he
doesn't seem to have a much clearer idea of the town than
I do. This morning the two of us are making the journey
there together. We are driving through the leafy white
suburbs of the capital, he and I, and we are heading North.

From Nairobi, we must drive around the side of Mount
Kenya and a way beyond. You turn a corner, I think,
about seven hours later, and suddenly the whole world
seems to stretch out before you. There are dark mountains
on either side and in front, a vast, shimmering, golden
plain. In the middle of the plain, a thousand miles away,
is a little white dot. It is the most important building in
Isiolo. The only man-made object of any beauty there at
all. It is the mosque.

'The DC turned to Saudi Arabia for aid,' says Mr
O'Rourke, 'and they gave us a mosque.' He laughs. I
laugh. But the mosque is a delight. It turns out, anyway,
that Mr O'Rourke has his information wrong. The building was apparently a present from an individual. It looks
beautiful against the big, blue sky. It is well used.

The town consists, more or less, of the one main street,
which is tarmaced and crowded with people. There are a
million children, shouting and running in hot orange jerseys and bright green shorts. There are long-limbed adults

2

in less of a hurry. There is a pile of broken down lorries by the entrance to the boys' school. And there is the dust.

Mr O'Rourke is keen to get home. He has tried to find the girls' school for me but he has failed. He knows his way from Nairobi to the hospital, which is a mile or so out of town. He does his shopping in a mzungu supermarket about a hundred kilometres away. There is only one street, really, in Isiolo, but Mr O'Rourke can't find the school.

He lives alone in his bungalow. He bagged the space when the hospital was still only on paper, said he would only take the job on condition that his house was built exactly on that spot. The spot has an incredible view (more plains, more mountains) but he's been living on it for three years now and it still looks like he's putting up with the place for the night.

In the corner of the sitting room are three dirty fish tanks. He points to the fish and for a moment his weary, philosophical voice finds a little animation. 'The females are generally dull coloured,' he says, 'but I found one with red on her belly so I bred her with the most colourful male. That,' he points to the smallest and dirtiest tank of all, 'is the result.' The result is dull. Far duller than the other fish. 'It's been my biggest disappointment . . . I spent a lot of time with those fish when I first came up here. There was absolutely mmm all else to do.'

*

Mr and Mrs Sweet, (he is a colleague of a friend of a friend of a friend and my main contact in Kenya. I will be staying with him until I find a place of my own) live in a long, luxurious bungalow similar, only without the guards' hut and servants' quarters, to any number in suburban

3

Britain. It is set about two miles from the main street.

'They've fenced themselves off,' says Mr O'Rourke as the two of us drive up towards the house. He is referring to the wire that divides the Sweets' garden from their neighbours'. The two houses are identical; both belong to white families. They are the best buildings in the town and they are in the middle of nowhere. There are the two Surrey houses, with the lawns, the fence that separates them off. And the desert. A thousand miles of nothingness. It looks absurd.

'They don't speak,' says Mr O'Rourke. 'The Jacksons prefer not to.'

Jim and Ann Sweet are an edgy pair. She is thin and worn, in her early forties, nervous, ever so welcoming; quite a comfort actually, under the circumstances. Her husband is tall and thin and fit. He's grey, about the same age, wears glasses and a beard and there's something about him that gives me the creeps. They live alone – or, alone with their servants. Mr Sweet works for the Livestock Development, is in charge of distributing small sums of (British government) money to struggling, local enterprises.

The evening is tense. We drink South African wine from matching, earthenware mugs and Mrs Sweet shows us a candle in the shape of an owl that she and her daughter (away at boarding school) picked up in Nairobi a week ago.

After dinner we move over to the sofa. Mrs Sweet brings us coffee. Mr Sweet goes a little wild in the presence, I think, of a fresh-fleshed mzungu female and offers the men a glass of brandy. Mrs Sweet shows us some photographs of the kids.

'I don't think they'll be interested in all your family

4

snaps,' says her husband and the photographs are put away.

It is ten o'clock and it's time for bed. Mr Sweet will take me to the school tomorrow. Mrs Sweet will wake me at seven with a cup of tea. I am bewildered by this hospitality. It is quite obvious that in real life we would disapprove of each other completely.

*

The school is not hard to find. It's up a dirt track off the main road. There is a sign. Isiolo Girls' School, a large, expensive wrought-iron fence, another dirt track cutting through yet more golden plain. There are some girls in school uniform scything the plain, very slowly. There's no rush. It's a big plain. Other girls are lolling about, lying under trees, watching the world go by, and the front three bungalows are filled with students. It is silent. The teachers, for some reason, speak in whispers. Some of the children are asleep because, already, it is very hot. The rest of them occasionally break the silence with lazy recitals, I think, of the verb To Be.

Esther Kathurima, a Christian, a Meru, a short and bee-like headmistress, ambles across the plain to meet us. She doesn't look me in the eye and her handshake is disconcertingly limp. She is not delighted to see me, but then it is very hot.

'This is the girl who wrote to you,' says Jim Sweet, though I don't know why he thinks I can't say it just as well. Blacks and women; he sort of holds the conversation with himself.

She laughs, looks at me, but still without moving her head, without bodily inconvenience of any kind. 'And I

5

didn't write back,' she says. 'Come into my office and we'll talk about what you can do.'

Sweet leads the way. The two of them talk over my head for a while. Then she turns to me, asks me again what I'm able to teach.

'Well . . . I suppose I'd probably be best at teaching English.' Very English. Mr Sweet interrupts.

'Daisy's come here to help. She doesn't want to be paid. She just wants to HELP.'

Oh Christ, this is embarrassing. I don't want to HELP; not particularly. I want to get away from Ladbroke Grove. I am a lucky girl and I want an adventure. You know, I'm BORED. But the headmistress is still smiling.

'First,' she says, 'thank you for your concern.'

Oh no. This is excruciating. I have no concern. Ms Kathurima is gently bored and, I dare say, irritated by the suggestion that I should. So I shrug, like a sulky adolescent and look at the floor.

She says she'll have a meeting with her English teacher and talk to me again tomorrow morning.

*

Sweet lets me out of his monster car, British government car – only the aid workers seem to have cars that actually work in this part of the world – and we arrange to meet at his office, along the main street, in a couple of hours' time.

Within seconds a tall boy called Peter introduces himself and offers to be my guide. He is nineteen – around there – speaks fluent English and is waiting to get enough money together to go back to school. I believe him.

Peter shows me the market. He shows me the place

around the back of the market where Somalis and Samburus make their daggers. I don't want to buy a dagger, but I tell everyone, with a fatuous, eager-beaver grin, that I intend to be around for some time and that I will buy several daggers before I go.

*

I am a Western girl and I have never been anywhere as poor as this in my life. I have never visited the Third World, and I am not happy. I am rather frightened. The dagger-makers are dressed like story-book warriors. They carry spears. Some of them have enormous – tennis ball-sized – holes in their earlobes. And there is this smell . . . I will grow to love it, in fact. I feel nostalgic for it as I write; it's a sour, stale smell of animal fat and human sweat and freshly cured leather. It makes me feel sick as I stand there, grinning. The smell, and the old man by the fire who is welcoming me, who doesn't have a foot. I am lost. But the children shout mzungu! mzungu! and roar with laughter and we all keep on smiling.

My guide leads me to a grass hut somewhere, somewhere around the back of the market. I am lost (in fact I never found this hut again, in all the time I was in Isiolo). There is an old woman lying on her side, and two younger women, one squatting by the door, the other by the fire. She is removing a dirty kettle, handing me a dirty glass, offering me something to drink. Oh JESUS . . . Do I have to? There are a thousand children at my feet, the women are smiling, Peter is gulping his down. So I drink. It's lukewarm, spicy, very sweet. It's fine.

But should I pay for it?

Would I cause offence if I offered to pay for it?

7

Then my guide jumps up and I follow him. Our hosts don't speak English. At the door I ask him if I should give them some money. He laughs. Of course not. Absolutely not. So I smile and wave and move on.

We sit down on an edge back in the main street and smoke a cigarette. Pete shows me a love letter sent to him by a Japanese girl. She is quite angry. He hasn't written back to her for several months now. She wants to know what's happening between them and she's coming to Kenya in May to find out.

'She will pay for me to go back to school,' he says, and puts the letter away.

Pause. He is bored by me. He is absolutely bored by me and it is rather disconcerting.

I don't exist.

What the hell is going on here? But then I suppose he doesn't exist either. We do not have a tremendous amount in common. Pause.

'I will pay for the teas,' he says, staring off into the distance.

'What? I thought you said —'

'Don't worry, ha ha. Don't worry. I pay for it.'

'No, no. For heaven's sake, I have to pay. How much did it cost?'

He won't tell me. Just goes on laughing. Brings out a handful of bangles.

Isiolo is famous for nothing. It's in the middle of nowhere. It's very hot and very dusty and there's not much going on there. A handful of air-conditioned vans pass through the town during the high season, but they don't stop for longer than it takes to fill up with petrol. They're all on their way further north, to the luxury safari lodges in

Samburu and Turkana. They will have a very comfortable holiday and on their way through Isiolo their drivers will stop at the garage. It's the last one for many, many miles. And Peter and a handful of other boys will tap on the luxury windows and ask the tourists inside if they want to buy any bangles. Most, I think (but perhaps I am biased), of the bangles to be found in Kenya, will have started life in Isiolo. You can buy them here for a tenth of what they cost in Nairobi.

What I'm trying to say is that Isiolo may not have much going for it – it's not beautiful, it really isn't beautiful, it's not anything, just a ramshackle town in the middle of nowhere – but it does make good bangles. Go to the craft market in Nairobi and they'll look at your wrist and say —

Ah ha. Isiolo bangles.

If you've been living there for the last six months it will give you a great deal of pleasure.

Anyway, Peter is laughing. I am faint with embarrassment. He is offering me the bangles, but I don't want to buy any yet. No, I say. No, I don't want any bangles. Let me pay for the tea and maybe I'll buy bangles later on. He laughs, won't tell me what the tea cost, so I hand him 20ksh. He takes it, puts the bangles away, stares back into the distance and maybe I don't exist any more.

I am very, very hot.

*

Jim Sweet of the Livestock Division works in a small room off a busy courtyard at the end of town. A handful of whites – caricature colonial types – with monster cars, out-dated, middle-class accents and safari shorts, manage not to mingle as they hang around with the hundreds of Africans there. His office is simple; its cracked, rather grubby walls are covered in dusty maps of the area. He has a tidy desk and a computer with the cover left on. In the top, right-hand drawer of his desk he keeps a tin of Nescafé. A Thermos flask, carefully prepared for him each morning by his servant, and handed to him by his wife, is filled with milky water. He offers you coffee when you go to see him. He has a spare plastic cup in the same drawer as the Nescafé.

I find him sitting at his desk – with the stainless steel pen – and a cold, hard air of importance. The visitors trickle in. He jokes a bit with a large and stupid looking British fellow who is dressed in khaki shorts and shin-length Doctor Martens.

'Of course back then it was different,' he shouts, at army officer decibels, and with the accent, 'but ne-ow it's the fashion to talk about *systems*.'

Jim Sweet plays with his pen and nods wisely. The colonial moves off, is replaced by an elderly African with a hat, a bald head and a smooth, stupid-looking face. He has written a letter to the Livestock Development to ask for a grant to buy some cattle. For some reason he isn't eligible. Sweet explains the problem to him with special patience.

He brings out the letter; plays with it and his stainless steel pen throughout the interview. At no point does he look at the man in the hat. He is polite, but there is this hardness in his voice, this hideous patience. It's uncomfortable – creepy – to watch.

Another African, a small, intense looking man in glasses, comes into the office and takes a chair against the wall to wait his turn. 'Explain to this man would you,' says Sweet to the newcomer, 'that we offer small amounts of money for specific projects to specific groups who are in greater need than he is, and who have already done a bit for themselves.' The new man translates and the old one gets up to go.

'I'll come back and try again later,' he says (in Swahili) and Jim Sweet allows himself a smile.

*

The Sweets are lending me their daughter's bicycle. 'You're very small,' says Sweet, very slowly. 'You shouldn't do it any harm.' I spend the afternoon reinforcing its tyres – and congratulating myself on finding such a rustic, no-nonsense pastime. I think of my friends in their London offices and feel so smug that I forget to concentrate on the job. Now I have broken an important part of both wheels.

Sweet drives home early to check on my work. Mrs Sweet hovers nervously and he shouts at her for the damage I've caused.

'Well, actually, she didn't really have anything to do with it,' I say, bravely. But it doesn't seem to make any difference.

*

My eight o'clock meeting with Miss Kathurima doesn't happen until half past ten. I sit on the steps outside her office, smoking cigarettes in an ankle-length, semi-transparent skirt which I'd decided was sexy back in London and I think nothing of it. A young and breath-takingly beautiful student, wearing white trousers under her skirt and a veil on her head, waits most of the two and a half hours with me. She sits there, quite silent and quite still and she doesn't look at me once. An older woman comes in to wash the floor. The student stands, moves the furniture back so the woman can clean more easily, sits again. I smile at her, but she looks straight through me and the minutes tick by and it is very hot and very quiet.

Miss Kathurima is cool during our meeting. Clearly, she is not desperate for my concern. There is a problem, she says. Two of the four classes I'm supposed to be teaching haven't turned up for school yet. She's given the pupils more time so they can get the term's fees together (all secondary education in Kenya has to be paid for). There is no point in my teaching to an empty classroom. I had better go away and come back in a week.

*

Back on the main street Peter greets me like an old friend. I don't like him (because he was bored by me) but still, I am delighted to have someone to talk to. A thin Somali boy with one and a half arms comes to join us. We drink sodas and talk – me with desperate, boiling hot liberal enthusiasm, they with coolly hot boredom – about the usual things: the World Cup, Gary Lineker, Bros. It is marginally tiresome for all of us, I think. Peter gives me a bracelet which I do not want. I take it off before I reach the Sweets' house, because I can't bear the prospect of his patronising questions. I'd told him yesterday that I'd given Peter 20ksh for the tea and he'd said, 'Yes, that seems like a reasonable fee for the service.'

*

A few more hours, then, getting nowhere with the Sweets' bloody bicycle – I think I've now ripped the inner tube – and it's time to watch the sun go down. We sit on the Sweets' verandah drinking gin and tonics and waiting for Bill, a short, fat American Peace Corps boy with a limp, who is to be my housemate. Mrs Sweet passes me a second gin and tonic and congratulates me on my ability to adapt to the colonial life-style so quickly and I laugh, because I am her guest, and I blush, because I am a liberal, and I wish that I'd thought to ask for a beer.

Bill arrives an hour late and without an apology. The Sweets are irritated. They have been making slightly bitter suggestions about starting without him for almost forty-five minutes; they make one or two more once he's arrived, but he is busy clapping an old servant on the back, making a great show of it, speaking Swahili even worse than I do, with an extraordinary American drawl, asking the servant, 'harrbaarree?' – which isn't how it's supposed to sound at all. The servant looks ill at ease, but he smiles. Bill says Ow-kaye and his eyes move off to another place in the room. He is a noisy boy.

But he seems to know his way around. He isn't like the Sweets who, from what I can gather, could just as well be living in Swindon (if it weren't for the servants) for all the contact their private life has with the African world. Bill dominates the conversation, reacts to anybody else's input with a peculiarly defensive and disinterested 'Ow-kaye' and, like Mr Sweet, seems to find it easier to look elsewhere when he is talking to you. He is also quite ugly, a little disfigured – he looks as though something went slightly wrong. His legs are far, far too short for his body. But I am optimistic. I assume that we shall be friends.

13

So he talks about me to the master of the house and the wife and I sit quietly. 'Bring her round Wednesday afternoon,'he says (to the sideboard). Mr Sweet looks at his earthenware mug and says, 'Wednesday would suit her fine.' Meanwhile Mrs Sweet and I take the coffee cups into the kitchen.

*

Every time Bill stands up he reminds me of how short and fat he is, and every time it is a surprise. He seems to be extraordinarily self-confident, considering how ugly he is. Maybe it's something to do with America.

His place is fine. By Isiolo standards it's a palace. There is a large, dark sitting room with a cement, red-painted floor. There's a lav, running water, electricity. Three bedrooms. It's great, actually far greater (space-wise) than anything I could afford in London, and it nestles in what I understand to be the smarter quarter of the town, amongst wandering cows and donkeys, tethered goats, car rubble and deserted building sites.

Our neighbours' bungalow is a good deal smaller than ours. Hundreds of people seem to live in there; a mother, a father, a sister and her husband, another woman and a grandmother, I think, and maybe eleven, maybe sixteen children. They are Arab Moslems, so there is a lot of conversation about the Gulf War. I heard Bill last night, in flirtatious mode, standing outside by the basin where we wash our clothes:

'Oh come aarn, Arrmerd, who started it? Who invaded Kuwait first?'

Our neighbours have relations out there. Achmed, the husband, has a brother staying with him who left Iraq a week before fighting began. The household has a television and a radio and ever since the war started Achmed, who drives a lorry, has downed tools completely. He and his brother spend all day and all night chewing miraa and listening to the news. The news is quite relentless. When there's none to be had on the English channels they tune into Swahili, then into Iraqi, then back to the English again.

*

I met the mother, Fauzia, earlier on today. She sat on the floor of their sitting room/bedroom with various aunts and children around her. Four more children slept on a bunk bed in the corner of the room. Achmed sat watching the telly. She was putting pink, sugar-coated fruit stones into plastic bags, passing the bags on to another woman who closed them up with a candle. The stones had come from an uncle in Mombasa. They were to be sold by an aunt who runs a hoteli in Wajir. Fauzia gave me a bag. They tasted pretty pointless I thought, but perhaps they are a delicacy.

*

So I am sitting in my big, dark, empty bungalow, hearing the news bulletins and the chickens and the children from next door; occasionally having them all drowned out by the cry of a passing donkey. I am sitting here, perhaps feeling a little lonely, wondering how I should go about making some friends, realising that Bill isn't going to be as helpful as I'd thought he would be, and Peter comes to call. It wouldn't have been hard for him to find out where

I live. It's a small town. Bill and I are, I think, the only whites who live in the middle of it.

'Perhaps,' he says, 'when you come back from the weekend you will give me a cassette.' I say I won't and he doesn't seem to mind.

*

It was stiflingly hot today. A gust of wind blew up the main street and for a moment I thought I was in Hollywood. With all the dust and the heat and the open road and the scruffy wooden bungalows, Isiolo looks exactly like something out of a cowboy film.

*

If you follow the main road through the town and out towards the new hospital, you will soon arrive at a police check: a few men are snoozing in a hut, a strip of metal with spikes sticking out of it is stretched across the road in front of them. There will generally be a small crowd of people milling about up there; selling more bracelets (though nobody will want them; the BP station happened a mile back), selling mangoes and bananas, whatever happens to be in season.

A tarmac line crosses the road at the checkpoint. It is the last bit of tarmac drivers will be seeing for some time. Beyond it lie thousands and thousands of miles of dust, bumpy track, peculiar tribespeople in story book costumes (or no costumes), snakes, lions, elephants and zebras. The track stretches straight into the horizon, for as far as the eye can see. There is bush and track and dark mountain and more bush and more track, and it is hard to imagine, looking out there towards it, in no hurry, watching the sun go down, that it would ever come to an end. The same road will take you, if you have the stomach for it, all the way up to the now impassable Ethiopian border. But be warned; it's a dangerous route. Drivers are not allowed to use it after dark (the reason for the checkpoint) without a police escort. Ethiopia is never far off, relatively speaking. Nor is Somalia. It is the Somali bandits who are feared the most.

Isiolo town works as an important market place, as a link between the vast wilderness of the North, and the rest of Kenya. I'll slip in a statistic here – very quickly – to give you some idea. First, look at your map. Find my town. Look north and see nothing. See, also, half the land mass of Kenya. Out of a population of nearly 24 million, only around 800,000 people live to the north of Isiolo. Out there it is nomad land. The Turkana, wiry, angry looking people, who carry spears and wear rows of heavily beaded necklaces; the Boran, half Kenyan, half Ethiopian and quite beautiful; the Somali Kenyans, who have softer hair, paler skin, long limbs and fine bone structures, who are among the most striking people I have ever seen; the Samburu (of Thesiger fame), who wear red and white, shave their hair off, also carry spears and have large holes in their ears – these are the people who live north of Isiolo. They live off their cattle and their camels. They bring livestock to Isiolo market and the town is filled with them.

To the south of Isiolo, around Mount Kenya, the land becomes much less barren. This is where the Meru belong. It is they who have the land for growing coffee and, more importantly, at least to Isiolo, the land for growing miraa. The Meru are generally more developed than the northern tribespeople; they're also richer. They have the worst drinking problem of any tribe in Kenya, and they don't wear funny clothes. Merus are better adapted to a Western system and, as a result, they are in the process of taking over Isiolo. All the big buildings are owned by Merus. They are not a popular crowd.

And of course there are the Indians, richer, I think, than the Kikuyu (who are among the most hated and certainly the most powerful tribe in Kenya; Kenyatta was a Kikuyu) and even more unpopular. There is a handful of Indians in my town; they're wealthy, seem to keep themselves to themselves. One of them, Bill's best friend in the area, is building an enormous house right opposite ours. Whenever it is finished it will be the grandest house in Isiolo by miles.

*

Isiolo is ugly and chaotic. It's dusty and hot as hell. There are nasty smells, diseased-looking donkeys, children shouting mzungu! wherever you go. It's lonely out here, but then . . . I think of a particular coffee shop in a particular shopping mall in a little town back home called Taunton, and – I swear to you – my heart almost explodes with joy. Isiolo is alive. I am happy to be here.

*

I have spent most of the afternoon lying on my bed feeling faint and waiting for the sun to go down. Of course it won't do. I must try to find the track which takes me back to the town. It's not far, maybe a five or six minute walk. Up until now, though, I haven't managed to do it without losing my way. There is a group of women somewhere between here and the main street. They lie under a scrappy little tree, during daylight, selling mangoes and bananas and they're very friendly, never in a hurry. They teach me a new word in Swahili every time I pass. Now, when they see me coming, they begin to laugh. If it looks like I'm coming from the house, they will point me in the direction of the town; but it's the bit from the tree to the house that's really difficult. Sometimes, when I look very lost, they will lead me all the way home.

So. First, I must find the tree. I stumble across building sites – you can't imagine the heat. I am pathetically nervous of the roaming cows and I take long detours to avoid them, only to turn a corner and be confronted by another. But I find the town eventually. And now I must have a rest.

I have been advised by Bill, and by the Sweets, that it would probably work in my interests if I avoided the bars altogether. There are a lot of Moslems here. The women under the tree have already told me off about the transparency of my skirt, though I haven't taken them seriously yet. Bill has already refused to take me miraa-chewing with his friends. 'Sorry, Daisy,' he says, 'girls don't do it here unless they're – cheap – you know? If you want to do it you're going to have to do it in the house.'

Well, I can't tell the difference between a hoteli and a bar. Not from the outside, anyway. Besides, dammit, if I want to go into a bar I bloody well will . . . So, I summon my sad, misguided courage and walk into the first place I can see. I have spent the last few minutes rehearsing 'Please may I have some tea?' in Swahili. I manage it. The woman behind the counter, dressed, rather disconcertingly, in a grubby doctor's coat, seems to understand, but she doesn't reply. She beckons me from behind the counter and leads me out of the back door, through a butcher's shop, past a skinny donkey and into another room with tables, only this one looks – and smells – all together more unpleasant.

It's boiling in there. I'm pouring with sweat. Actually, I think I may be about to faint, and I've forgotten how to ask for tea in Swahili. The place is filthy: there are flies on the tables – the air is thick with them; they're bursting through the hatch that opens into the kitchen. I say 'tea', finally, and collapse onto a greasy chair. They give it to me, and I drink, and feel proud for having managed it, out of something so dirty, in front of so many staring children and in such a disgusting room.

*

Bill and an Indian man – not the one who is building the palace, but another, who has two thumbs on one hand and a very nice, old fashioned pick-up truck – are waiting for me when I get back to the house. This is my first weekend since arriving in Kenya (I moved into Bill's house a few days ago) and Bill appears to have softened. He is going to a Peace Corps reunion weekend about a hundred kilometres away. Last night he asked me if I'd like to come along and was rather put out, I think, when I said yes. The Indian is giving us a lift halfway there and I am keeping them waiting.

The journey is tricky, only because Bill is so nervous, I think, that I am going to rape him. Conversation doesn't flow and he still won't look me in the eye. The other Americans are serious and hospitable and friendly, in a disinfected, disengaged sort of way. They make matey jokes (they know they're being a bit naughty) about the Kenyan man's dislike of hard work, and they talk about their own work with great care and earnestness. They tell me a bit about the country and it becomes clear that none of them like it very much, although our plain hostess, Bonny, who has messages from Jesus pinned up on the walls of her house, and who doesn't drink, and who won't allow her guests to drink because it will shock the neighbours, manages to work up some warmth for the mama at the market who sells her papaya for a special price.

We eat spaghetti, made with a ghastly party spirit and a lot of tinned tomato puree. It's all jolly good innocent fun – it's a nightmare and the spaghetti is disgusting – and then we play some party games, giggle about David's lavvy troubles and go to bed.

At lunch the following day we meet up with a middle-aged volunteer called Cecille. She wears butterfly spectacles and she has lipstick all over her face. She looks like a exhausted tart in a bad film, but everybody greets her with more hearty warmth. She's obviously the woman of the moment.

Loadsalarfs, then, for all of us, as we fill in a make-shift lottery form which has something to do with the American Superbowl.

It is a grim weekend.

*

Bill and I are picked up for the last leg of our journey home by a Kenyan in a suit with a briefcase and a big car. He says he's a businessman, but when asked what kind, is evasive:

'I build things,' he says. 'All sorts of things.'

The journey is only about fifteen minutes long. By the twelfth minute he admits that he isn't a businessman at all. 'I'll see you tomorrow or the next day, so I'll tell you the truth,' he says. He is the head of security for Isiolo.

Apparently there was a murder a couple of houses up from ours the week before I arrived. An old Arab man was panga'd to death by a gang of thieves. 'There has been a terrible rise in thuggery these past few months,' he told us. But murder, in the town at least, is unusual. 'Isiolo's OK,' he says, 'but the people are very good at doing a lot of nothing.'

* * *

Bill has a theory that one of Achmed's sister-in-laws has a crush on him. It seems hard to believe. She came round this afternoon with her four-year-old cousin and we sat on the sofa drinking tea. Bill played pat-a-cake with the baby while she and I discussed the size of Africa (there was a large map above her head), and her forthcoming marriage. She is waiting for her father, who keeps a shop in the desert further north, to find her a husband. She giggled when I asked her if she was looking forward to it, and covered her face with her hands. I think she is looking forward to it a great deal. Otherwise, I'm not at all sure what she does all day. A lot of nothing, I suspect.

* * *

I wake up this morning, absurdly early, to the deafening sound of rain. The house is creaking under the strain and water is pouring through the ceiling and windows. Bill has cooked me some French toast. His family sends him maple syrup in gallon bottles and he is very generous with it. I must remember to like him.

The rain has turned the dust into glue. I try to walk into town with my shoes on, but they break under the weight of the glue – each footstep brings with it another boulder of clay until eventually your leg can't pull the weight. Either that, or the shoe snaps. The air is filled with horrible insects and I'm not convinced, as I stand there, that I'm going in the right direction. But I have to move. I can't stay there forever, and even though the mud must be riddled with the sorts of animals which climb up through the soles of your feet, and I'm clearly going to die, I take my shoes off and keep walking. My skin is itching and I'm lost. An old woman walks past me, stares at my naked feet and laughs. 'Mzuri sana,' she says, 'now you are like an African.' And I smile, but the smile gives me cheek-ache.

*

The man behind the counter at Barclay's bank (the second most beautiful building in town) knew my initials and account number before I had even told him my name. Isiolo is a very small town and I suppose I am fairly distinctive. It's lovely in the bank. There's air conditioning, and white walls and cushioned seats. I think I'll be spending lots of time in there.

*

It takes two and a half hours to put a call through to England. The postmaster asks me, once I've paid him, why I wanted a personal instead of a 'station' call. A station call costs half the price. The reason, of course, is that I didn't know. But there you have it.

The postmaster's wife sits opposite her husband, on the same side of the desk as me. She doesn't talk much, she just rests her head in her hands and watches her husband work. Every now and then his telephone rings. 'I am expecting an international call,' he says, and it echoes across the red cement floor and people in the queues turn to stare at me, 'I don't want anyone on this line for even one minute.' Then he talks for a bit, about other lines to be called, how they could be called, and what business needs to be discussed on them once called. And his wife rests her head and listens. He is friendly, but then so is everybody.

*

Maria and Zuleka, two sixteen-year-old Moslem girls on their lunch hour from primary school, find me wandering around in search of the house and lead me home. They wake up Henry from his resting place in the building site next door. Henry is the watch for our and several other houses. He speaks very little English and my Swahili isn't up to much, so we find it hard to communicate. I don't have keys to the house, but Henry does, so every time I trip off on another hopeful and pointless jaunt, I have to call him.

He's not a very good guard, but he's friendly and it must be a boring job. He spends most of the time, as I said, sleeping in a deserted building site just behind the house. My need to wake him every time I go out under-lines the pointlessness of my outings and the whole thing has become quite embarrassing. I've learnt to say 'Sorry', in Swahili, which I feel is very useful, so I say that a lot, when I find him, and otherwise try to stay out of his way.

Anyway, my new friends aren't so diffident. He arrives faster to their call than he does to mine and we go inside for tea. They are wearing bright orange jerseys and I wish I knew how to ask them if they're not too hot.

They don't like the tea. I have yet to learn how to make it Swahili-style. We sit on the sofa below the map and talk about nothing for a while. They are very shy, particularly Maria, the plainer of the two, so there are a number of pauses. I'm delighted to have company, but it's so hot and I need to lie down. They show me the henna patterns on their hands and nails and we giggle politely. Zuleka brings some paper-wrapped powder out of one of her pockets – she produces it shiftily, when I have turned away – and the two of them smear it onto their faces, spill a little onto their skirts.

Then Hassan turns up. Hassan. Hassan sells bangles down at the BP, but only sometimes. He seems to have a very pleasant life. He lives well, does an awful lot of nothing and drops in on Bill almost every day. He is long and thin; young, say about nineteen, and most of his family live up in the north. He has an open, intelligent face and he is always laughing. Occasionally you catch a glimmer of meanness there, a sort of ruthlessness, when he's discussing prices or bangles – or both. Yet he is easy and friendly, on the whole. His English is totally ungrammatical, but he is fluent.

He came round to call yesterday and Bill asked him to clean the mud off his company bike, which he did. I don't know why; perhaps at least partially from the boredom. Bill is supposed to be a Peace Corps boy and, as he tells me so often, one of the American volunteer's most important duties is to try to bridge the cultural gap; to make friends with the people around them, to learn to respect . . . I don't know. Bill seems to have a peculiar way of going about it. Whatever, Hassan came around yesterday and sort of stayed. He sat under the map and told me how much he hated the Indians, about how much he wanted to kill them, about how he was going to be rich one day.

So – Hassan turns up and the two girls suddenly become very quiet. They look at the floor. They won't acknowledge him at all. When he speaks to them they refuse to hear and they leave soon afterwards.

Which is more than Hassan does. One of his seven brothers has been to Sweden, he says, and he wants to go himself. When he was a child he was kidnapped by an aunt, apparently, or a grandmother, and taken to Madrid. But then somebody else kidnapped him back and now he is in Isiolo. He told Bill, who reported it back to me with tremendous glee, because he doesn't like Africa though he would never admit to it, that Hassan didn't want to go back to school because then he would be rich and he would have to support his family. He said one of his brothers had made it to university, but that he had then been forced to emigrate to Australia in order to escape from his grabbing cousins. Bill was delighted of course, because Hassan's tale demonstrated yet another insurmountable weakness in the structure of the non–American dream (he's incredibly patriotic, you should hear him talking about this bloody war). But I don't know about Hassan right now. I don't know about anybody. Out here I am a baby. And I need to learn fast.

*

Bill tells me we are invited to dinner by Kabede, an Ethiopian doctor who lives around the corner with his wife, mother and four children. They rent a small bungalow, which must be about a quarter the size of ours. There are probably ten bungalows on the plot and I think those ten are among the most envied in town.

The sitting room is small and crowded. Its cement floor is unpainted; its ceiling is made from uncovered corrugated iron. The day's sun makes the place feel like an oven, but it has a certain cosiness, I think.

Conversation, before Kabede and the children come home, is a little stilted. Bill says 'uh-huh, owe-kaye', but that's pretty much as far as it goes. The wife, slow, fat, poised and beautiful, has offered us chai which we sip politely. I am feeling neurotic about my knees (are they indecent? Can she see them?), about everything, really. There is a limit to how many times one can say mzuri about a cup of tea. So I look at the crowded walls. Kitsch paintings of Jesus, large Ethiopian Tourist Board posters encouraging visitors to enjoy 'thirteen months of sunshine'. But Ethiopia is in chaos at the moment (it's only a few months before Addis falls); travellers are not allowed in. Above the door which leads, I assume from the burning giko in the corridor, to the kitchen, is a coy portrait of a pretty little white boy doing nothing, looking demure, smiling. It's a professional photograph, torn, perhaps, from a colour magazine. It seems peculiar, now. It seems more peculiar still when I meet Kabede.

The Doctor comes in and his mother, a wiry, dignified looking woman dressed from head to toe in muslin begins to talk. Up until now she has lain, silent and motionless, on the sofa watching television. She doesn't speak Swahili or English. She is staying here until it is safe to rejoin the rest of her family in Ethiopia. Meanwhile she watches a television she doesn't understand, smiles and says mzuri. It is hard to imagine what goes on beneath it all, the smiles, the yards of muslin —

Kabede is abrupt. He suggests that while I am waiting for the school job to work out I might like to teach his four children. I'm delighted. It gives me something to do, some point of contact in this strange town.

He talks to us about the history of Ethiopia, about his dislike of the English – of whites in general. He tells Bill how much he preferred the last Peace Corps boy posted here to him. The last boy, he says, became an African. Isiolo loved him. He was a good man, everybody's friend, spoke Swahili fluently. Bill on the other hand is cold and distant, keeps himself apart from the rest of the town, is very much a white man.

Tee hee hee. Bill is livid. He has to be polite, of course, because of the tea, and the delicious smells coming from the kitchen. But he broods, keeps referring back to it, finally gives Kabede a ponderous explanation which is rounded off with a ghastly smile, a humorous shake of the head, a: 'Sawe you see, Cabootty, I can't be friends with everybody in Isiolar. I choose my friends just the same way as he did and, y'know, some people are going to be offended.'

But Kabede isn't interested in Bill. He is more interested in when we are going to leave. So he asks us. Oh dear. A misunderstanding. There is to be no supper for us tonight. Kabede denies there ever was an invitation and we are turfed out into the darkness and the glue. I have promised to come and call tomorrow to discuss lessons for the children.

Today is not a busy day. I write some letters – always a good time-killer – and on the way to the post office I meet a couple of fat-thighed English boys who are doing exercises with the British army just north of Isiolo. I tell them I am living with a Peace Corps boy and one of them says, 'Oh-oh. Don't want to meet him. He's bound to be against the war.' Big joke. They tell me they're waiting to be sent to Iraq, that 'there's no time to be frightened', whatever that means, that they come to Isiolo occasionally to go to the disco.

Hassan told me yesterday that the army people were horrible: 'They say fuck this, piss that all the time. St. Very stupid.' He's probably right, but the boys are pleasant enough to me.

★

Mrs Sweet turns up at the post office in her great big car and offers me a lift back to her house. I am supposed to be mending the bicycle today.

She stops off at the butcher on the way home to buy fresh bones for her dogs. (She and her husband get their own meat in the same place Mr O'Rourke gets his. They do not shop in Isiolo if they can help it.) And I wait in the car.

Meanwhile a skinny old Turkana man limps by. He sees a bone the size of my little finger lying in the dust. It has a scrap of yellowing meat hanging off it and he bends to pick it up. Mrs Sweet is nipping back towards the car as he puts it in his mouth, chews it, moves along the way.

Still, as she skips, a child approaches the open window.

Says, 'Give.'

He stares at me as Mrs Sweet pops back into the driving seat. She brings out her purse, clicks her tongue, 'You leave Isiolo considerably poorer than you come in,' she says and hands him a shilling.

We return to luxury. After only a few days in Isiolo her house already feels like a little haven, like an isolated patch of unreality. I suppose that's what it is. She offers me lunch – warm bread rolls, lettuce, cheese, those sorts of things – and I can't possibly refuse although I have eaten (goat stew and chapati) an hour earlier.

Isaiah, Mr and Mrs Sweet's effeminate young gardener, is skipping about nervously in a crisp green overall. He is too deferential for comfort but I try to hold a conversation with him in my useless Swahili. He is just telling me about the banana tree when Mrs Sweet comes hurrying from the house. 'Daisy,' she says, 'shouldn't you be doing that bicycle?' And I suppose I should, but it is unlike her to be so assertive. Isaiah is sent to the front garden to water the lawn. He drops everything, jumps and runs.

I bicycle back from the Sweets' house through the town and I am accompanied by gales of laughter from every direction. It is odd to be at the centre of so very much attention. And all I seem to have to do in return is smile. One begins to understand how easy it is to be a member of the Royal Family.

*

Hassan comes to supper and teaches me how to cook chai. He puts in too much sugar but neither of us mentions it.

*

I spend the morning eating mangoes and the afternoon with a belly-ache in bed. Later on I amble into town, bump into Peter who is ambling also, looking as under-occupied as I am. We amble together though we have nowhere to go and very little to say to one another . Peter breaks the silence with:

'Isiolo is bored today.'

I look at Isiolo and I suppose he is right. People seem to be waiting or sitting or lying in wheelbarrows – even more aimlessly than they usually do.

We go to the Isiolo Hoteli to drink tea. It is hot and crowded and painted a sickly mixture of green and brown. Samburu men (spears resting beside them), Turkana women (babies at their breasts), groups of Somali women dressed in brightly coloured headshawls, Somali men in turbans and kikoys, all sit with their chai and their plates of ugali and some of them stare, but most look straight at their plates.

The room is large and dark and people's voices rebound off the hard furniture and dirty walls. The burning gikos (and the burning sun outside) help to make the dankness sweat. But there is a vitality here; waiters thump glasses in front of you within seconds of your sitting down. If you order food (and there is only ever one dish, whatever the blackboard may say) it arrives immediately, great big bowlfuls of it, steaming hot and sinking under a thick layer of fat. Like the smell of the warrior, Isiolo Hoteli is an acquired taste. I will grow to love it.

A man called Japan who is eating bananas at the next-door table comes to join us. He must be forty-odd. He has grey hair and a child-like, flirtatious manner. I am pleased to meet him today.

*

Mr Job joins Bill and me, again at the Isiolo Hoteli. He wants Bill's help to export the jewellery he makes to the United States. Bill is gruff, because he generally is, and especially gruff because he is eating. Mr Job is friendly, earnest, determined. He pays for our dinner. Bill says 'He-ay, I'm a volunteer. Nobardy who's a volunteer refuses a free gift.' A friend of Mr Job's comes up to tell us that ten US army people have been killed in Saudi Arabia. Mr Job says, 'So what? They have caused many deaths', and I look at him.

Later he laughs. 'Did I hurt your feelings,' he asks, 'when I said "So what"?' He doesn't like the English much, like most people around here it seems, but he knows an English couple in Nairobi who, he hopes, may help to get him an export licence. 'They are very proud,' he says. I think he means rude.

Bill and I are walking back towards the house and Mr Job says he will accompany us. The walk, he comments, is sometimes dangerous after dark. Bill is still gruff. I dare say he is irritated. We bump into Achmed, our next-door neighbour, who is taking a handful of his children into town so they can telephone their mother. Fauzia has recently been sick. Her husband has sent her to stay with a sister who keeps a cafe in Wamba so she can rest. It appears that she is unwilling to return.

Achmed, who is large and fat and humorous, tells Bill, with the clear intention to bait, that ten thousand American men have been killed in Saudi Arabia. Bill says, 'Naaar, Arrmed. It's teyen. Not teyen tharsand.' The exchange is amicable enough. We will go round to his place and watch the news later on.

*

There are four of us watching television: three men and me. I don't think the women are allowed to sit in the same room as the men, especially when there are male visitors. The three men chew and smoke and offer me cigarettes and I say Oooh no, asante sana, and cross my legs and feel dainty and bogus and a little out of place. In the corner, four children are asleep on a bunk bed. They look something like Miss Haversham's wedding cake, the beds and the still children and the mosquito net shrouding them all.

*

Two young girls stop me as I bicycle home today by blocking the path and holding out their hands towards mine. The thinner, apparently more intelligent of the two asks me for money and I refuse. They follow me home and into the sitting room so I offer them some tea. The thin one disappears for a while. I am loathe to follow her in case she might think I'm thinking – as indeed I am thinking – that she's robbing me. But I follow her eventually, dead friendly grimace on my face, with a hearty laugh etcetera and am ashamed of my suspicions when I discover she is doing the washing up. I ask her not to, several times, but she refuses to stop.

'I want to help,' she says and turns, with a cloth, towards the food cupboard.

Meanwhile her sister is learning to ride Bill's bicycle in the sitting room. I am embarrassed, very embarrassed by the clever girl's determination to help. And they won't drink any tea and everything's awful. When the girl in the kitchen has finished her cleaning she returns to the sitting room.

'Now I am go,' she says, and we say goodbye, me with some relief and her, it turns out, with half the contents of my cupboard.

★

Bill, who has been out to dinner and, to be fair, has earlier been quite friendly and apologetic about how he couldn't take me etc, returns home fairly early. He goes into the kitchen and starts knocking around with a few pans. Within minutes Achmed has come out of his house to talk to him.

'Bill!' he says from over the garden fence, 'what are you making?'

I feel a little jealous, I suppose, because I have been alone all evening. I have been feeling isolated and listless and I have been wondering what the hell I'm doing here. I have been wishing I was a boy; things are a good deal easier for a boy in Isiolo.

But Achmed is a Moslem man, and though he has been nothing but friendly and jovial and welcoming I can't help feeling nervous of him. I can't believe that he wouldn't disapprove of everything about me, and I am in his country, living beside his children and his wife. Whatever, he too, it appears, has been lonely this evening. Presumably he is missing his wife. Bill goes out to talk to him and I stand in the kitchen, eager for conversation of any kind, trying to summon up the courage to go out there and join them. Then . . .

'Neeaaw, we did naart starrt it. Who invaded Kuwait?'
'Who started bombing Iraq?'

'Irarrq hayas taken harstages today.'

'Oh, nooo. You've been listening to the propaganda.'

I wonder, do I imagine it, or are their flirtatious squabbles developing a bit of an edge?

★

I am up early this morning, which makes the day longer. I have a meeting with the headmistress. My classes, it turns out, still haven't turned up. 'Nobody does anything in a hurry here,' she says. 'They will probably wait until the deadline.' Then she tells me about my clothes. She is extremely embarrassed:

'They're a little bit – how can I say this? I hope you won't be offended . . . Here, come here, bring your chair closer so I can explain.'

My clothes are too transparent.

'The children haven't been so exposed, you see,' she says. 'They will be looking at your clothes and not paying attention to the lesson.' She laughs. 'I also notice that you smoke. Now, I have no problem with that. No problem at all, but maybe if I came to your country and I behaved as I do at home, people might find certain aspects of my behavior – erm – unpleasant. You will find the people are very narrow here.' She pauses, watches her hands make a narrow gesture, 'Simply because they have not been exposed, you see?'

And I think of the time, our second meeting, when I had to wait for so long; I sat on the steps at the front of the school, in a skirt that could have been made of tissue paper. I sat on the step and smoked cigarette after cigarette. I remember her coming out briefly and asking me if I wouldn't be more comfortable on a chair inside,

35

and I squirm. I squirm now, as I write, thinking again how embarrassed she must have been, how she had clearly never really wanted me at the school in the first place . . .

So I am sent away again. But I will be back, still trying, in the most decent clothes I can muster, toothpaste in my mouth to cover the smell of smoke. I will be back at 7.40 on Monday morning.

*

Isiolo is very quiet today. It was pay-day yesterday and I am told that the town has a hangover. I take breakfast in a cafe, because I want to get out of the house and I don't want Bill to think I'll be hanging around him all day. When I come back to the bungalow its entire front is draped with large, grey underpants, 1 to 9, some of them with old brown stains in the gusset – they're hanging right across the front of the house.

'It's washing day today,' says Bill as he watched me fight my way through them.

Around the corner I find two young, very shy girls on their hands and knees washing the master's bedroom floor. Bill asks the thin one if she would like some food, but she pretends not to hear him. He touches her arm, mimes eating and says 'food' in Swahili. She recoils, then giggles. She won't answer though, not until Bill gives up asking and I give it a try.

I cook them fried eggs, toast and tomatoes. They send the eggs back; they want them all stirred up. They leave the tomatoes, say they don't like toast, that they want bread. I have a little trouble with that. Bill says 'that's owkaye', because he sees I'm looking irritable, and it doesn't help. I think they are being rude and of course I'm being silly. Anyway, we shake hands very warmly after the second attempt at breakfast, and I remember the filthy underpants across the front and my heart goes out to them after all.

*

Kabede the doctor accosts me from his regular standing point, a high cement step outside the clinic.

'What happened to you?' he says.

I tell him I've been trying to find his house ever since the last time we met, which is almost true, but he doesn't look convinced. He leads me into a back room behind the clinic and tells me to get started. I find four children and a neat, serious looking man sitting at a table with school books before them. It's a little awkward. They are being taught already. He is teaching them English.

He works at the local primary school and knows far better what he is about, but I sit down, am handed a pineapple by one of the children, which I put on my lap, and we begin. There seems to be no fixed ending to the lesson. Two hours later I am still there. The children (all girls, between the ages, say, of nine and fourteen) only titter each time I speak. They can't understand my accent. I don't know how to explain why something is right or wrong and the thing is a drag. I'm feeling claustrophobic. I'm wondering when I'm ever going to be freed.

Finally, the serious man closes his books. We, the teachers, have a grown-up conversation with Kabede about our progress. I wonder if I am stepping on the neat man's toes, but Kabede doesn't. He says he expects he will see me at the same time tomorrow and I say he probably will, because he is very overpowering. But then he shakes my hand and smiles and says thank you and I feel grand and the whole, rather fatuous, scheme takes on a new and more important meaning.

★

I have learnt the word for meat in Swahili and so I have decided to venture away from the Isiolo Hoteli where a few of the waiters speak English and get myself some goat stew and chapati in a new establishment. So here I am, very hungry and very hot, of course. The waiter is beaming down on me, beaming and waiting, waiting —

'Tafadhali – er- k-nya – er kula- nay? Nyanya?'

And I've forgotten it. I've forgotten the word – I can't even remember it now, I've had a total block about the bloody word ever since. Anyway, so I mime someone eating meat, say 'stew!', look eager, look hungry, look encouraging . . . So does he, but he doesn't understand. He runs off nodding. Perhaps he has gone to find someone who will be able to help us. But he hasn't. I wait . . . and wait. Nothing. I beckon him over again. Again he runs; still he smiles.

'Meat and chapati, tafadhali,' I say.

'No chicken.'

'OK. Acuna matata. Goat.'

He runs off. He returns.

'No chicken.'

'OK. Mzuri sana. What about goat? Or any meat? Nipe meat. I don't mind. Acuna matata.'

He runs away again and I wait. And wait. And wait. It's fine, of course. I have nothing else to do. I ask again. He smiles, runs to the cash desk and leaves the room.

He returns a few minutes later with a tin of cherry jam and makes me an enormous – I mean five inches worth of – sandwich, gives it to me in triumph and I say 'Delicious'. Mzuri mzuri. Mzuri sana. And I think again of how very white I am. I laugh but it makes me feel lonely.

★

Wanjella, a young man with very ugly lips – they stretch from jawbone to jawbone, from nose to chin and seem to have no sense of co-ordination – greets me like an old friend, though I have no memory of meeting him before. Anyway, we have bumped into each other here at the Bomen, the smartest hotel in town. It is the only place where I dare to drink alcohol. It sells ice; when you're feeling rich it even sells cheeseburgers. Sometimes it's a relief to go there, though it's musty and overpriced, really. Shoddy finery, whatever the expression is, but sometimes it's a relief to see another white face. Sometimes, when you're feeling lonely and the goat stew has lost its tantalising call, a bit of mzungu food, a few vegetables, can work wonders. And so, of course, can a few bottles of beer.

Wanjella says, 'But Daissy, you look very good today.'

'I say, 'No, I think I look just the same.'

He looks closer. 'But your face – don't you use a mosquito net? You will get malaria very soon. Don't take the pills until you get it. Malaria can be very dangerous. When will you come to dinner?'

I don't know about Wanjella. I don't know if he's married or what. He is very good at English, I know that. And he has ugly lips. I think I will do a little research before I make a date. Better to be safe, isn't that right? Even when you're desperate.

★

The disco is playing again. It is so silent here. I must be a mile away from it, but I can hear the scratches in the records. Achmed and co went to bed long ago. I wonder where Bill is? I have eaten that pineapple. I have a belly ache. And now I will go to bed.

★

The two schoolgirls, Zulecha and Maria, the ones who led me home, who put white powder on their faces, have come to call. They bring with them various babies, cousins, siblings, I don't know what. We sit on the sofa. I offer them tea. They refuse. I offer them mango. They refuse. I have nothing else to offer – except a seat outside, but they laugh at the suggestion. Bill is out there playing Monopoly with Achmed and two of his co-workers. Zulecha knows one of them but she doesn't go out to say hello.

'I am a-*fraid*,' she says and giggles and covers her face with her hands and turns her face to the wall.

After twenty minutes of silence (they won't talk, not even about the wretched map, not with the men outside, but they won't leave and they won't eat anything), they invite me round to Zulecha's place. I am keen to go.

Zulecha lives over the road from me, in a much poorer house than Maria's. They are related in some way, the two of them, but I can't get to the bottom of how. It keeps changing. Perhaps Maria is Zulecha's aunt, perhaps her sister. Perhaps they share a father or I don't know what,

40

but they are both Moslem and they are never seen apart.

Zulecha's mother, a large, unsmiling woman with a ferocious face, is washing at the tap outside as I arrive. She doesn't welcome me much. She talks in Swahili, though I later discover she speaks English perfectly. We go to the sitting room ahead of her, and after she has finished washing she walks straight on through to the room beyond.

The sitting room is cramped and very clean. It has an old cassette player, an odd assortment of half-broken chairs (car seats) all covered in purple and white crôchéd doilies, the cement floor, the tin roof – children everywhere of course, and there is a cupboard stuffed full of social science books. There is a large photograph of Jerusalem on the wall.

So we are sitting around staring into space, me saying mzuri sana about the tea, the crôchéd circles, the picture of Jerusalem, and in comes the terrifying mama. Her enormous body is covered, except for a big, fat, powerful shoulder, in layers of electric pink. I see her daughter quail. I quail, still I try to smile.

'Golly', I say, 'how fast you *knit* grandmama'.

It's awful. She doesn't want me here. Perhaps she thinks I'm patronising her. Perhaps I am. She is educated and intelligent and she doesn't want me here. But I want her to be my friend. Maybe next time. I get up to leave and my escorts are clearly offended.

'So you are not happy here?' Zulecha says.

Oh, I am, I say, I am, but the question doesn't help. 'I have to go, though. I have to . . .' Panic. I have to go and there is no excuse.

The two girls have sat mute ever since the mother walked in. Their demand that I stay seems unreasonable, but of course that is beside the point. It's a different kind of reason out here I think. Everything's topsy turvy —

Maria solves the problem by inviting us to her sister's house, which is directly opposite. We get up to go and all three of us, I think, though nothing is said – in English at least – breathe a glorious sigh of release.

*

Maria's sister's house, where Maria lives, is very luxurious. There is a telly, a video, a picture of lions made from nylon carpet hanging on the wall and a brand new three-piece suite. The sitting room is smothered in crôchéd circles; the ferocious mama's purple and white affairs look quite dreary by comparison.

Relations loll on every surface; young men chew miraa and stare. More chai. More mzuri's. Zaidi, mistress of the palace, is fat, warm, laid back, hospitable. She has been keeping Maria for several months now, ever since their father, a Boran civil servant, left his city job and retired to the country. He and his wife rejoined their nomadic cousins and are wandering the desert somewhere between here and Addis Ababa. Maria must stay in Isiolo to be educated.

Zaidi pulls her two-year-old from her breast (he has a tantrum) and goes in search of an instruction leaflet sent to her from New York by an old English teacher, who claims to have designed a solar oven which can be made from a cardboard box. It would be useful for the women around here who are forced, so I'm told, to wander further and further afield for their firewood.

I don't know why Zaidi has asked me to build it for her. She is an educated, well-off woman; she would be just as capable of doing it as I am – probably more so, actually.

Whatever, you can imagine that I am delighted. I want Zaidi to be my friend. I want to have something to do, something that will involve me with as many people in Isiolo as possible. And, of course, if the oven works it could indeed be extremely useful. The landscape is littered with women – children, geriatrics (always female) – weighed down by the weight of half a broken up tree.

I take the instructions away and say to Zaidi that I will return tomorrow, when she is less busy, to discuss it further. She is a little bemused, perhaps. I think, in retrospect, that she rather hoped I would take the instructions and not bother her again until the oven was tried and tested, up and ready for mass production. Too bad. I wasn't going to do that, although of course there is nothing to discuss, and I wouldn't do it now.

*

I have been locked out of the house. Henry, the sleeping watchman, is nowhere to be seen and neither is Bill. Achmed invites me into his place. We drink chai and eat delicious sweetmeats and talk about the war. He offers me a cigarette, which I should refuse but can't, and asks me if it's true. Am I really a cousin of Bill's?

Bill is a tricky customer. The Peace Corps pays for his house. At first he didn't really want me living in it, but then he thought he might be able to make some money out of me, which he does because I pay him rent, so he changed his mind. He has told me I mustn't mention the rent to anybody because they'll be shocked (and anyway it could get him into trouble. Against Peace Corps rules, I think). He also tells me that we must pretend we are cousins. He says, and I believe him, that most people would be outraged if they thought an unrelated girl and boy were living, unchaperoned, in the same house. It's reasonable enough. Also our living together might mess up his sex life (about which, more later). And that, too, is reasonable enough.

But Achmed is a friend of his. Bill eats in his house almost every day. Achmed is a strict Moslem, but he knows that things are done differently in my part of the world – which explains why he has offered me a smoke. So I am sitting in Achmed's house, drinking his chai, smoking his cigarettes. He's asking me – and he's laughing, because Bill hasn't convinced him – whether or not it is true. Are we really related?

What can I do? Well, I lie of course, but it's not comfortable. I am angry with Bill for forcing me into this position. I am angry with him for being such a carefree crook towards someone who is supposed to be a friend. And on top of that the inhospitable, greedy, fat, ugly bastard has locked me out of the house. God knows when I'll be able to get back in again.

*

I am told by Zaidi that Esther Kathurima has applied for a transfer. She is engaged to a man in Meru and she wants to go and join him there. I'm terrifically happy for her etcetera etcetera, of course, but I don't know how it will affect my prospects for a job . . .

*

I get to the school at 7.40 to find the staff room locked.

'Nobody is here yet, Madam', says one of the students. She smiles, shrugs. 'They're justie late.' She goes off to find a key to the staff room door. I leave my bicycle in there and follow her to the front of the school. She shows me a chair, put down there for my benefit, which looks out towards the miles of plain. She gestures towards it, says, 'Justie you relax', smiles again and disappears.

I try, but it is a little awkward. The chair has been put on the cement platform where before I sat chain-smoking in a transparent skirt. I can't smoke and I don't know what to do with my big, white hands. The girls are staring at me, smiling, being incredibly polite and I cross my legs, uncross them, lean forward, lean back, but no teachers arrive. So I wait.

Another girl approaches and explains that the school is about to have assembly. It assembles itself – there must be about two hundred, maybe four hundred pupils – whatever. A respectable number, at least. They lope across the grass towards a naked flagpole about a hundred yards from my chair. Understand, as you imagine this, the soft blue light, the coolness of the morning, the muted sound of voices on a thousand miles of golden plain. Imagine the children's loping, the easy grace, the lack of hurry. Understand that there are no teachers here, no visible form of discipline at all, and listen . . .

The school, in blue and white, makes a messy huddle beneath the flagpole. One girl stands out before them and they sing a song – haphazardly – with no energy at all. When the song is over a group of ten or twelve girls emerge from the ranks, make a scruffy march around the flagpole. The ranks are silent. Somebody raises the flag;

the march rejoins the gaggle and assembly is over. Back over the grass, to lessons.

But still no teachers are here. The pupils sit in their classrooms and wait for the day to begin.

I go to the staff room (corrugated iron roof, blackboard, desks, cement floor, gushing tap – they never did get it mended – cracked walls, silence) and finally somebody arrives. Then another and another. But nobody has seen the headmistress.

'Perhaps she has gone on safari,' says the science teacher.

An hour later she still hasn't turned up. I go to the reception room outside her office and find the deputy, Mrs Tacho, an Indian Moslem, sitting in the head-mistress's chair. Fifteen students all of whom from what I can gather are trying to get off non-existent lessons sick, an old man in a hat, a father and daughter with a suitcase, are awaiting her attention.

I am allowed to jump the queue, am offered a seat in front of Mrs Tacho's and asked to wait while she finishes talking to her husband on the telephone.

'One little thing goes wrong and you are angry with everyone,' she is saying. 'We went to Meru and we were happy, but . . . well, it's good to hear you laughing.'

Only twenty-three of the expected hundred pupils have turned up. They are to be grouped into one class and taught together.

I start tomorrow.

*

Behind the Mandeleo Hoteli, beside the three-storey building site which has been deserted ever since the outlawing of the ivory trade – it was to have been

46

magnificent, but its builder was forced into hiding – lies a courtyard. Somali traders rent the tiny rooms surrounding it by the day. They sell electrical goods there, nasty denim trousers, ugly Western nonsense and also some of the most beautiful fabrics I have ever seen.

Everything comes from – I'm not quite sure where actually, but it's been smuggled across war-torn Somali borders, and its traders are real-live villains. At least I think they are. They look the part.

I walk from the main street, up a long dingy corridor and I am struck by the noise. After the dusty slothfulness of midday Isiolo town the activity is vaguely disorientating.

I stand in the middle of the courtyard and the cries – Sssst! Wé! Sista! Here!' – can be heard from every one of the tiny surrounding cells. I have come with Peter, who is looking humorous and laid back, saying, 'Pole pole' (gently does it, take it easy) and leading me towards a cell in the far corner of the yard.

Inside an old, sick man is lying on a bed, coughing his belly out, gasping for breath. Another man is asleep on a bed beside him. From outside come the calls of 'Sista!', and a gang of people have followed me into the room. It is very crowded. It takes a while to adjust to the light. But there, amidst all the dirt and coughing is a pile of the finest, most delicate material in the world. It's like something out of a fairy tale. These materials, when you pick them up, they are so fine they can't fall to the floor. There are pinks and purples and greens and oranges and reds – and a million people grabbing you from behind. And sweat and dankness and the dying man, gagging, in his final breath, demanding exorbitant prices he couldn't possibly expect me to pay.

But I buy a little and pay a fairly exorbitant price. It seems cruel to haggle with a man who can't breathe, and his friend, or his nephew, I don't know what – he's a long, thin, sickly boy – wraps it all up very carefully in newspaper.

'We give you special price because you are volunteer,' he says. 'Maybe you teach my sista or my cousin.' And I know he hasn't given me a special price. Of course he hasn't. But his words are like magic to me. I think, well then, perhaps I am not so unwelcome here after all. And I walk away quite proud to be alive.

*

I arrive at the school a little late. Neither the English teacher nor the head or the deputy is there. The other teachers can't help me and I am a little tired of hanging around. I want to get started. So I ask someone which is the first year class and go in there to introduce myself.

There is no desk or chair behind which to camouflage my general awkwardness, so I stand at the front of the class while the students talk amongst themselves and I wonder what the hell to do next. Somebody gives me a table. I say:

'OK,' but I've never spoken in front of so many people before – or at least not when I can see their faces. My voice is trembling.

And the class breaks, in unison, into a cat-call 'Heeelleoe Meeeaaaam. Hiii. Hiii theeeyeeer Meeeyaam' and they roar with laughter and it's terrifying. I smile (can't trust the voice) and pull a teacher's look of mock surprise. They are quiet eventually. One of them explains that the last mzungu at school had been an American. Simple as that.

So I stop feeling paranoid, say: 'OK, ha ha. Anyway – I – am – from – Great – Britain – and – I – have – come – to – teach – you – English. Turntopageone.'

But nobody has been given any books. I go away to find some and bump into Esther Kathurima, just rolling up for work.

'Ah –' she says. 'Come in.'

There is a problem. She has mentioned me in passing to the DO – equivalent, I suppose, to a mayor – and he is adamant that under no circumstances should I go anywhere near the school, literally, until the Board of Governors has discussed it and agreed to give me their permission. The next Board of Governor meeting isn't for another fortnight . . .

So off I go again, back down the dusty road, back through the wrought-iron fence, back to the town and to eating too much goat stew and to nothingness.

*

A more tactful, less insensitive person, I feel you thinking, would perhaps have taken the headmistress's very kind and gently worded hint and moved off to find work elsewhere. A little self-justification is needed here. I'm unwanted but I want to stay.

What can I say?

I could make some sort of attempt at appearing to care. It's true that the classes at school tend to suffer from a lack of teaching, but whether that's due to lack of funds, lack of teachers or lack of discipline on the part of the headmistress on her staff, I have yet to find out. It's certainly true that these children, whose parents, for the most part, have scraped together the fees at unimaginable sacrifice, spend most of their days, from what I can gather, with their heads on their desks, fast asleep or waiting for a teacher to turn up. That's true.

It's also true that I like it here, that I like the school, I have an aquaintance or two, a solar oven to build. It's also true that I don't like travelling around without a purpose. I like to make a base.

And, the school did make vague, unofficial noises (to somebody else) while I was in London, indicating that they wouldn't object to my teaching there.

I am aware of my whiteness, the fact that the school may feel patronised, that the teachers may feel, although I'm not asking to be paid, that I am treading on their toes, that I am white and interfering. I am aware of all that, but perhaps not aware enough. I do not want to move on. I'm quite settled now. I will move, I think, only if I am forced to.

Oh, God. Well what would you have done?

*

But I am a little depressed. Goat stew doesn't take my fancy and nor does the lonely bungalow. I head for the Bomen where I am joined by lazy Peter. And this time, for the first time, we have something to discuss. I tell him all my troubles and he suggests that I go further out into the bush. North of Isiolo, he says, people don't bother with stupid things like Boards of Governors. He is convinced, he says, that if we go back to his home town of Marsabit, I will have no problem in finding a job. He says he will take me to his old secondary school and introduce me to his teachers. He is sure they will be delighted to have me. He says:

50

'We go now.'

And finishes his soda. I think to myself that I have two weeks in which to do nothing. It would be a good time to see the North, even without the prospect of a job at the end of it. To travel with someone who knows his way around would be excellent. But Peter; he's tricky. I've not the faintest idea what goes on behind the laid back, humorous manner. I don't fancy him and I don't want him thinking I'm thinking . . .

SEX.

Raises its ugly head. I need time to consider.

So I laugh and say something idiotic about there being no hurry in Isiolo. I tell him I have a few things to do, which is clearly not the case, and that I'll come to find him at the BP station tomorrow morning. Perhaps we could head off in the afternoon.

*

Mama Fatima, her big, fat shoulder covered up today, seems to be in an altogether better frame of mind. We walk back from the town together, call in on an aunt of hers along the way.

Another crowded room, another chai, more men look-ing gormless, doing nothing, chewing miraa and spitting the ends on the floor.

These men, they do seem to have it absurdly easy. One of the men at Fatima's auntie's place will later become a friend, of sorts. But today I see him, his moronic, lazy face, his unsophisticated stare and my good, liberal heart is a little tried. I want to shake him. The lot of them. All the ones with dicks.

I find Kabede at his usual post, standing with his usual impatient, irritable, slightly frustrated air. He is middle-aged, slim, with a sharp eye and a surprisingly relaxing grin. There is something about him which makes one want his approval. He has a great deal of charm, but then he can suddenly be quite unpleasant. He makes me a little nervous.

Anyway, I tell him I shan't be teaching his children for a week or two after all. And today he is not abrupt; he is extremely charming. He takes my side against Kenya's, says the Board of Governors are very stupid, that if he were in charge he would give me a job at once.

It sounds unimportant now, but at the time it was a great comfort. There was something very pleasing about having something to discuss with someone in the town – some kind of business to transact. And there was something delightful about Kabede taking my side.

★

I was planning to ask Hassan about Peter, but he hasn't turned up today, so I am reduced to Bill. The idea of discussing sex with Bill makes me feel a little queasy, but it has to be done. I ask him what he thinks about my going off with Peter and he says he doesn't know Peter, that I can go or not. It's up to me.

Well, I know. But does he think it's sensible? He's been around Isiolo for longer. Bill is no help at all. He's annoying me. I decide to go.

★

A bad night. I have spent the whole of it trying to work out a way of telling Peter that I don't want us to shag. How can I do it without causing offence? But I must before we leave. I must make it clear.

So I bicycle down to the BP. Peter is lolling about. He jumps up when he sees me. He is carrying a small, brown, plastic vanity case and he looks quite alive.

'Shall we go then?' I say, and he says:

'Yes. Yes.' It's a free lift to see his family. A free jaunt away from the dusty town. Of course he is enthusiastic.

'I'll – er – I'll go and pack then, shall I?'

'Yes. Hurry. Quick. We get Wamba bus.'

'Listen, Peter, you realise, don't you, that we'd be going as friends. That's all. Just good friends.' And it's so indirect and bloody English it's a wonder he understands what I'm getting at. But he does. He looks at my purple face and maybe that's a pointer, and he begins to laugh. Right from the bottom of his belly, he begins to laugh.

I try a smile, but the embarrassment is too much. My lips refuse to move.

'Just good friends,' he says, His whole body shakes. 'No problem. Yes, yes. No problem. Just good friends,' and he turns away. 'I wait,' he says. 'Come here when you're ready.'

And I bicycle back to the house.

*

The Wamba bus goes without us in the end. So we wander around town looking for a car which might be going in the same direction. It shouldn't be hard; as I have said, there is only one road through Isiolo. Traffic can only either be

53

coming from Wamba or going towards it. Everybody, except the aid workers and the luxury safari vans, is quite friendly about offering lifts. We are not worried.

Peter goes off on his own, comes back saying he's found a Land Rover which will take us but that we might have to wait a while so the driver, who is charging us for the journey, can fill up with as many people as possible.

We go to sit in the car. And we wait. An hour passes and it already seems to be very full. Two hours pass and the car is ridiculously full. We sit. And the sun beats down. And the driver rests his bottom on top of his bonnet, chews and discusses the war. Three hours. The car is so hot and so crowded that it has now become impossible to move and – if not impossible, at least very unpleasant – to breathe. The driver keeps chewing. The passengers stare into space. Four hours and I am growing impatient.

I swallow my pride and ask Peter if he thinks we'll be leaving soon. He laughs. Tells me not to worry. We stare back into space.

At last the driver gets up from the bonnet. Everybody climbs out of the car to give it a push start. We move, about a hundred yards, stop again. The wheel is changed. Another push start and we're off. The journey over the rough and dusty Ethiopia-bound road, through the endless plain, under the burning sun, past zebras and antelope and nothingness, is to last three hours, though it is only forty kilometres long. Our driver stops every five or ten minutes to refill the engine with water.

About five kilometres away from Wamba we are stopped by a truckful of police going in the opposite direction. Three of the policemen want a lift, so they pile in, stick their rifles out of the window and we move on. The police take us to the police station, to report the driver for overloading, and the rest of us make our own way back to town.

*

Wamba makes Isiolo feel something like New York. It's small. There is the one street, but the town only runs along it for about fifty yards. There is no electricity and, I think, only one building (the post office) which isn't made of wood or mud. A deep ditch runs along either side of the road and at night, when it is quite dark and quite quiet, the ditch can prove a little troublesome.

There is nothing Western about Wamba. Hungry-looking Samburu stare at me, but they don't speak Swahili, so we can't communicate. Not, now I come to think of it, that they show any great signs of wanting to. They don't smile, either. It would be hard to miss the hostility. Wamba is beautiful but I am homesick for down the road. I wish I was in the Isiolo Hoteli eating goat stew and looking for friends to talk to.

Peter takes me to visit one of his sisters who is at primary school a few miles up the road. The school compound, except for the matron's lantern, is in complete darkness, but the children's shouts as they eat supper in the pitch black dining hut can be heard from miles around. The matron gives me a guided tour of the dormitory. Children crowd around me but I can't see their faces. The room is heavy with the students' enthusiasm and I keep bumping into bunk beds.

We return to the town to find some food but it's late – eightish, say – and there is nothing left in Wamba except cabbage. We eat in a filthy, stinking place whose only lamp is so dirty it might just as well not be burning. We cannot see what we are eating and neither of us can summon the energy to talk. We eat the cabbage and the cold, greasy chapati in silence, and we go to bed.

*

I've taken a diarrhoea pill so I don't have to go to the lav for the rest of this hellish journey. The lodge keeper directed me to his choo a few minutes ago. I put my hand out towards what I assumed to be the door handle and it wasn't. It was a five-inch long fucking cockroach and now my belly is heaving and my hand, which held it, is on fire and I think I'm going to be sick.

*

I am up before Peter. I go to a hoteli for tea and mandazi and who should appear from behind the kitchen wall but Fauzia, Achmed's wife, who is here to take a rest cure, you will remember, from her children and her husband's obsessive following of the Iraqi war. It is quite wonderful to see a familiar face, even if I'm not immediately able to put a name to it. There have been so many faces, and she's been away.

A crazy Samburu man, crying crocodile tears, comes limping into the cafe a little later. All he seems to want is for someone to say good morning to him, but nobody will. He turns to me as a last resort, I think, and when I reply he cheers up and goes away. Doesn't even ask for a cup of tea.

Then Peter comes in, sees Fauzia, pretends not to see me and sits at a separate table. I wonder if I have offended him and take offence myself. It's only later that I realise he is being tactful.

Fauzia, who looks no better now than she did in Isiolo, thin and frail and fine-boned and very beautiful, will not allow me to pay for my breakfast.

She is the kindest, holiest, humblest – and most humbling – woman I have ever met. I don't know this in Wamba. She strikes me as friendly and generous, that's all. But during the following months she will become a good friend, a great comfort, a teacher.

I say asante sana. Kwa heri. See you around.

*

The bus that was supposed to take us from Wamba to Marsabit has been cancelled indefinitely. Its driver was very drunk last night and there was a terrible crash. The bus is a write off. Nobody seems to know about the driver. They don't seem to mind much, either. His recklessness is notorious around here. He did Isiolo to Wamba in forty minutes last week. Well, and when you think it took Peter and me seven and a half hours . . .

So we are stranded. I hear there is a Catholic mission school about half a mile out of town. Who knows, they might like the idea of a short-term English teacher. I decide to give it a try.

Through the dust and the hungry children to a haven of elegance and wealth. The Catholic mission is built like an old-fashioned monastery, surrounded by flowers. Its cloisters have somehow managed to catch the only breeze in Kenya. I wait to be shown into the headmistress's office.

She's an old Italian woman – a nun, of course. She talks in a special nun's whisper, so I try to copy her, but to no avail. She doesn't want me there, not in the least. She only takes on volunteers who are willing to stay around for two years minimum. I feel a fool. What does she think my chances are of finding work further north? No chances, she says. None.

But perhaps I would like to meet her Domestic Science girl? She's from Britain. We are bound to get along. She stands up. It's the end of the interview. I follow her down the breezy cloister to the Domestic Science room. She knocks on the door. They talk in those whispers and out comes a short-haired Irish girl, about my age and dressed in mufti.

So is she a nun or isn't she? It makes a difference how you talk to her, doesn't it? She's not. She's just an ordinary Irish girl who's caught the whisper. Her family disapproves of her being out here. She has no friends – the school is too far from the town, the Italian nuns don't talk to her. She says she doesn't mind, that she works so hard (six and a half days a week, daylight hours) that she doesn't notice it any more. I think she is very brave.

We make polite conversation about this and that. I tell her that Peter has just scrounged a lot of money off me which he claims is for his sister's school fees. She says, 'I wouldn't stay around *him* for very long'.

We discuss other people's vegetable shopping habits. Some people, she says, will go to the market in the morning to buy tomatoes and then return in the afternoon because they've forgotten to get the potatoes.

Stupid, I say, and flick some more ash in her tidy sitting room. But that's how I spend all my days in Isiolo. I go backwards and forwards to the market and I'm loath, even, to buy all my tomatoes in one go.

She shows me a special plastic bag which she's filled

58

with water and hung outside her front door. It means she gets a hot shower every night. But now I must leave her. If ever she makes it to Isiolo she must come and call. 'Just ask for the mzungu girl,' I say, but I never see her again.

*

We find an empty truck whose driver claims to be heading for home so we climb in. At Archer's Post, which is honestly in the middle of nowhere – it makes *Wamba* look something like New York – the driver announces we must get out while he goes off to fill up with cattle. He says he'll be back soon.

Funny kind of soon. He returns three hours later, by which time it's dark, and the police at the checkpoint won't allow us through. There's no escort available, so we're stuck for the night.

We sleep on the floor beside the truck. Everyone thinks it's terrifically funny, this white girl sleeping on the floor beside a truck. But I ignore them; I've lost my sense of humour, can't see the joke at all. The driver makes a fatuous comment about wanting to marry me and I scowl. He's baiting me and I really hate him now, but there's nothing I can do. I pretend not to notice the laughter and that makes them laugh even louder. So. I'm at Archer's Post being laughed at by a bunch of loathsome strangers and I am longing for Ladbroke Grove.

*

What a delight to be back in Isiolo. I return to my bungalow to find two large and over-excited Americans just waking up. One of them has a shiny new army-camouflage–look sleeping bag spread over my bed. The other one, the fatter one, lies on the sitting room floor shouting out schedules and rolling a joint.

Chris and Jon, they're called. One of them's a city whizz-kid in Washington or New York who says he's forgotten how to use long hand and can only write with a pen if he's using capitals.

They're friends of Bill's, away from their high-pressured First World jobs for one month. They are here to catch the spirit of Africa. So they roll a joint.

'Her her,' says Jon to Chris, 'This is Africa, huh? *Stoned* and it's only nine-thirty in the morning!'

Half an hour later they are stuffing their safari trouser pockets with water melon and bitter apple flavoured bubblegum lollypops, brought over from Washington for the beggars in town.

They are off, they say, to have a look around. But Isiolo is small; they return too quickly. Chris is rolling another joint, and I wish it would have some effect. He is talking in urgent tones about the shower he plans for a couple of hours' time. But then Hassan joins us. He is delighted by the Americans; there is a greedy twinkle in his eye. And they are delighted by him, do a lot of flirtatious rigging; SAY, say their hearty, desperate laughs, we're getting on real well with an African. We can be boys together no matter what. And Hassan is playing along, giggling like a baby, introducing the subject of bangles each time the others pause for breath.

'Hassan,' says Jon, 'I want you to make me one hundred bangles. When can you do it by?' He turns to me, 'I'm gonna give 'em t'all my friends.' And where, I wonder, did he ever find so many?

*

I talk to Achmed over the garden fence, tell him a bit about the trip, about my meeting with his wife, give him the message to expect her back on Friday and his big fat humorous face lights up. We return to our various kitchens and I stare into space.

Five minutes later he is back. Am I sure that Fauzia will be returning on Friday? He wants to slaughter a goat to welcome her, so he needs to be sure. I say Oh yes, absolutely sure. Friday is tomorrow. The goat will need to be killed this afternoon.

The goat is slaughtered. A portion is given to us. Hassan comes round and teaches me how to make Somali goat stew. But Fauzia doesn't return on Friday. She doesn't return for a week.

*

There has been a great deal of talk about a man called Nassir. He was doing some sort of business deal which involved American aid money. A representative of the American Embassy is coming down to visit, to inspect their various projects, to talk with Nassir about the deal. But Nassir has disappeared. Nobody has seen him for six or seven weeks and Bill is furious.

I am sitting in the house one night. Hassan has been and gone. It's dark and very quiet and I am alone. There is a rattle at the gate. I know it's not Bill because he's gone off with the American boys on an Experience Africa jaunt. There is no noise from next door. They must have gone to bed. I am a little frightened.

The rattle grows more impatient. So I go out to see what's going on. A small, thin Somali man with extremely long eyelashes and a miraa pouch in his cheek glowers at me through the railings.

It is Nassir. Nassir has returned. He's pretty cool.

*

Zulecha and Maria come around again. Hassan, and the laid back and fascinating Nassir, are sitting outside with the Americans. The girls refuse to come in. We sit on the floor by the clothes washing tap on the opposite side of the house and I am feeling very irritable because they won't speak and I know there's more fun to be had with the gang on the other side. So we sit, and I want to shake them. They won't talk. Why have they come here? What's the point?

Maria breaks the silence. 'Push me home,' she says. And I do, gladly.

The brother of the Indian man who is building the palace opposite ours – the brother of Seileesh, Bill's best friend – joins the rest of us for supper. He won't eat the goat stew that Hassan made yesterday. He won't eat anything, because he doesn't trust mzungu cooking and he doesn't believe that the stew wasn't made by me.

Nassir sits above the rest of the group on a high stool. He says nothing. He watches us, and the pouch in his cheek grows fatter, and the pile of miraa debris at his feet grows higher. The brother, I never did get his name – and he always refused to recognise me when we saw each other afterwards, so he won't feature much – is angry with Seileesh. It turns out that it is he who is funding the construction of this ridiculous palace. His brother,

Seileesh, has only been contracted to build it. And he is not doing well:

'I told him three months ago that the workmen were bad. He's never there, and the Africans can't work unless they're made to. And he complains to my father that I'm interfering so I stop. Now, three months later, he comes to me. "These workmen are bad!" He wastes money, time, materials . . . My brother is a lazy man.'

He leaves.

'Oh, he's great,' says Jon. 'A real character. A typical Indian, y'know. Very abrupt. He doesn't really mean it.'

Seileesh turns up. He has with him a packet of Benson and Hedges and I say 'Good heavens. Golly. Benson and Hedges! Wherever did you manage to get those?'

'In Isiolo,' he says. He nods and lifts his fat hand to take a drag from the one he is smoking, and his golden bracelets jangle accompaniment. 'I can get them.' But he doesn't tell me where.

The group has gathered to discuss travel arrangements. Bill is taking more time off to show the American boys around more of East Africa. Nassir is to be their tour leader and Seileesh is coming along for the ride. He is charging $70 a day for the use of his car. The two tourists are bursting with energy. They want to go now and plan later. I think they have some kind of check list:

Elephants – seen
Get ripped off – to do
Tribespeople – tick.

Seileesh wants to plan for ever and ever.

The idea, I think, is to go off into the desert. I'm not sure. Whatever, everybody is being very boring and determined. Seileesh, who has that dogmatic manner common to so many stupid men, lays down the law and demands that the group divides its trip up and returns from the first jaunt within two or three days, so he can hire the car out to somebody else in between. The others have no choice but to concede. Nassir says nothing. He chews and watches – through the long eyelashes, from the high stool. And everybody ignores him.

*

Make the mistake of sharing a joint with the Americans. Stumble to bed and spend the rest of the night unable to move, paralysed by the usual fear and by the usual, agonising memory that I'm a fool.

What in God's name am I doing here?

Everyone else goes to the Bomen for beer.

*

PART TWO

I return today after an aimless two-week break travelling around the country.

I took the night train from Mombasa to Nairobi and woke up at dawn (from the cold – I was too mean to pay extra for bedding). The sun was breaking over those endless plains. The impala, wildebeest, zebra and giraffe paid no attention to the engine noise as we passed slowly by. They stood, apparently frozen, looking out towards the golden beginning of another day. It was a beautiful sight, and a beautiful omen, I decided in a rush of passion and sentimentality which could only have been brought on by such a view – for the rest of my stay. If not life. Today is my twenty-fourth birthday.

*

Isiolo is as hot and dusty as I left it. I am struggling through the town with a bicycle, a cabbage, a rucksack and a pair of eggs.

'Seesta!' calls a man I have never seen before. He is lying in a wheelbarrow. 'Seesta!' I smile, but he beckons me over. 'The short American,' he says, 'went that way.'

So the short American is back. Ah well.

*

Bill is not pleased to see me. He was not expecting me back so soon. There is something the matter. He's embarrassed. He's standing on one leg:

'There are some things you will never understand about this culture,' he says eventually. He has a woman coming round this evening. Would I mind hiding in my room while she is here? I say I'll do it, but she arrives early and I'm caught red-handed cooking goat stew in the kitchen. She doesn't stay for long. Is it me that has frightened her away, or the shortness of Bill's legs, the appalling, waxy grimace he wears when he's trying to be charming? I shall never know.

Isiolo seems to have picked up on the fact that I am here to stay. It is very gratifying. Now it takes twice as long to get to the market and back. There are so many conversations to be had. People I have never seen before stop me in the road:

'Seesta,' they say (or Madam), 'how is Mombasa? How is the safari? . . . Where is my giftie?' Or they say, 'Seesta! The Bill he went thatie way.' I always say thank you, because I'm well brought up, but I'm rarely looking for him.

*

Two men at the post office enquiry desk are in a state of great excitement. I have been away for a long time. Yesterday was my birthday and two telegrams have arrived. One of the men goes off to fetch them while the other spoils the surprise by reciting to me what he remembers of their contents. He knows them by heart.

'You are very happy,' he says as his colleague hands them over. And I am, and they seem to be too.

The woman who sells stamps, she's thin and pretty and flirtatious, wears a lot of well-accessoried bright colours, (today is a yellow day; yellow hair band, large, plastic yellow earrings, yellow necklace, yellow everything except for the shoes; she wears the same tatty old white shoes whatever the day) grabs me around the waist from behind.

'And we thought you were long gone,' she says, throwing her head back and giggling coquettishly. It's a bogus performance and I wish she would take her hands away. 'What?' she says, 'you came back yesterday and you didn't come to see us?' There is something about her that gives me the creeps, but she seems determined to make me her friend.

*

Bill is in a furious temper. The women's group has built a hoteli in the market place. They somehow managed to get together 7,500ksh (an average monthly wage in Isiolo, if you're lucky enough to have a job, is 500ksh – £10) in order to do it. Bill, who's been involved in the organisation, says he asked them before they started whether or not the project had been passed with the health people. The women's group said it had and went ahead. But Bill met the health man yesterday and double checked. Disaster. To have a hoteli in the market place is out of the question. Too many people are in hospital from eating bad Isiolo food as it is. Now the entire project has been brought to a standstill. The money has been wasted and the building must stand in the market place unused.

Had the women's group checked or not? Perhaps the health man changed his mind? Did Bill ask the women's group before building started whether or not the health man had been notified? Was Bill being officious? Who knows? Anyway, Bill is taking the incident as a personal affront, carrying himself like a martyr and mumbling a lot about not being able to get anything done in this country . . . Miss Kathurima's face does not light up when she sees me. 'So,' she says, 'you have come back?'

The board of school governors never did get around to meeting while I was away. They will meet on Saturday and I must go to see her again on Monday morning.

*

Hassan keeps telling me lies about the price of bracelets. He says that he sells them much cheaper than anyone else and I've discovered it simply isn't true. He is charging the young Americans ridiculous sums, but if they want to flash their money around – and it's not as if the saving would make much difference anyway – I don't see that I owe them any more loyalty than I do to Hassan – well then, I shan't say a thing. And I'll let Hassan know that I'm not saying a thing. I think that would be rather a clever move.

He comes around in the evening. The Americans are back from some jaunt or other, and the rigging begins. Bill doesn't tend to talk much with his friends. It's peculiar – they discuss plans, but there are no jokes between them, no ordinary, easy contact that I can see. Hassan is giggling like a baby again, but his eyes are half crazed with greed.

He knows I'm watching him, and he knows I know he's not being fair. But he gets what he wants in the end. The Americans don't seem to care. It has to be said they're a good-natured pair, if nothing else. They trade a handful of bracelets for a brand new pair of trainers. I've never seen such robbery.

Haggling is interrupted by occasional observations on life. Chris mentions blonde girls with tits and office travel profiles – apparently everybody has one. I don't really understand what he is talking about. Bill accuses Hassan of selling him fake amber. Bill has no tact. There is tension in the air. Then he tells the Americans that the girl with long hair who came calling yesterday has taken a fancy to Jon.

Hassan says, 'Ha ha. Very funny. Long hair today. Long hair last week. Always long hair'.

But he's sharp. He's young. He's not stupid.

*

I am killing the afternoon by riding around Isiolo in increasingly larger circles. I find myself down by the meat market and my bicycle conks out. Its gears have been going ever since the Sweets gave the bike to me, but I've never, in spite of the empty days, managed to be bothered to try to mend them. So I stop, fiddle around a bit, kick the front wheel a bit. A group of children have stopped to stare and the group is growing larger every minute. The heat. The children laugh each time I show a sign of impatience and I am feeling irritable.

A toothless old man approaches. He is dressed, like many Isiolo people, in rags: a pair of shorts that were made for a seven-year-old twenty years ago; they gape at the front, are tied together by a piece of bind-a-twine, no shoes and no shirt. He shouts at the children, attempts to shoo them away. They scatter. Regroup within seconds. He looks at my bicycle and I think Ha! What would he know? He asks me if I have a box of matches and I think Oh, yes. Here we go. He takes one of the matches, burns it, brings out another. Stuffs them into the gear box haphazardly, wherever they'll fit – and yet with great concentration.

And it works.

He smiles his gabby smile, nods, says, 'Aya, aya' which, translated, doesn't really mean much; uh-huh, perhaps, something like that. And he moves away.

I grow irritable too quickly here. I am ashamed. Again.

*

I cause offence in the market. Bump into the man with whom I have discussed buying a kanga several days ago. I have no money on me now and the man is angry. He says I promised I would buy a kanga from him today. I say I can't. He says (it's translated for me): 'You mzungus, you're all as hard as nails.'

And I think, yes. Perhaps he's right.

*

Seileesh drives the Americans, Bill and me up to Samburu National Park. We see the elephants and so forth and stop off at a luxury lodge for tea. Mzungus everywhere. And they are all so incredibly ugly. An old white man in shorts leans over his shiny-haired niece/daughter, whatever, explains to her how she should order tea:

'It's not like it is at home,' he says. 'Get it weak, with a bit of lemon and it's delicious. Mmm. I find it very refreshing.'

The manager of the lodge, he's a friend of Seileesh, tells us that Saddam Hussein has been assassinated. We believe him. The Americans are livid when they discover he's joking, say they realised it all along.

Back in Isiolo, the street children gather around the car to beg. But Chris, the fat one, who has learnt Swahili incredibly fast, gets in there first. Asks them for shillings before they get a chance to ask him.

Oh ho ho.

The children are astonished. One of them hands him a twenty cent coin. Oh *ho* ho. So Chris rewards him by paying him back, with a thousand per cent interest. Suddenly there are a hundred hands stretched out. Every one of them offering money.

'Hey, woa,' says Chris.

As we drive off he puts his hand in his pocket, brings out a handful of change and throws it out of the window. He watches the children scamper after it and the American boys share a laugh.

They aren't wicked, these Americans. They lack a layer of gentleness, perhaps. They're not my cup of tea.

*

Seileesh and the Americans are arguing about the route for the next jaunt. The Americans, in their own words, are determined to 'meet their objectives' (what did I say about a check list?). But Seileesh, who has been exhausted by Samburu – he seems to be exhausted by everything – who is not accompanying them on this trip anyway, wants to have the car back within the next couple of days. Seileesh wins.

*

The Americans have gone and so has my odious house mate. He woke me at six this morning to say that they were going to Mombasa – on the bus. It seems that the boys will be unable to meet their objectives after all. And now, of course, I rather miss them.

*

I branch out this morning and go to the Frontier Cafe for breakfast. It's on the Christian side of town, so it sells alcohol and on Friday nights it turns into a disco. The waiter gives me the bill. He has overcharged me.

Suddenly the battle of being white and rich and lonely in this god-awful town, in the middle of nowhere, over-whelms me. I must quibble over the five shillings for the egg I never had. I must always be on the look out, always smile. I must keep my temper, be polite, never relax, keep on smiling – because I'm white and rich and in the middle of nowhere. Because I have so many bloody advantages. But nobody seems to talk to me unless they're after some-thing. The children stare and say bicycle. The men stare and say bicycle and ask me if they can have it.

I took my Walkman out as far as the kiosk today. It's about a hundred yards down the road; sells milk and mangoes and so on – everything you could ever want except cigarettes. It's run, on and off, by the house girl of the father of the English teacher at school. She has a very girlish voice, but she is rarely there. It was pathetic.

I took the Walkman because I knew it would make people talk to me. And they did. The builders opposite (remember Seileesh's palace – it was supposed to be finished by now) called me over. They are always friendly, but today I was feeling sorry for myself. I knew why they had called me over. I planned that they should call me over, but then when they did, and they asked for my Walkman, I felt resentful.

Things will improve. I know they will. But it's hard to believe right now.

I spend the rest of the day on my own in the house. Too depressed and self-pitying to do anything but sit. And sit. The room is very dark, and it's growing darker and I have done nothing but sit.

Seileesh has been given a key. He gives me a fright when he breaks the wretched silence and jangles his bulk through the sitting room door. I don't recognise him. For some reason I decide he is Achmed and the conversation goes like this:

S: How are you after yesterday?

D: What? Oh great. It was great. Seileesh took us to Samburu. Buffalo Springs.

S: Yes.

D: We saw lots of elephants.

S: Yes. I'm exhausted. I am feeling ill.

D: Are you? Oh dear. Your wife was feeling ill before, wasn't she? Is she better?

S: What?

D: And so was Bill. He was feeling ill yesterday.

He leaves.

*

Hassan turns up to take me to his friend's curio shop three kilometres beyond the frontier. He borrows Bill's bike (it would make him furious – and I think he must somehow have found out about it, because although he never says anything, I notice he takes to keeping it padlocked afterwards, even though it's always left inside the house) and he bicycles way ahead of me. I lag behind. My bike is stuck in third gear and the road is riddled with pot holes. Sometimes I have to stop for a break. The children who are scattered along the road all the way throw stones at me and shout 'mzungu!'. It's what children do, I suppose, but this has not been a very good weekend.

The curio shop is closed, so we bicycle around – Hassan says for about sixteen kilometres, but then that could mean anything. And we bicycle home.

'Tonight,' he says, 'we will chew miraa'.

Now I have been told by Bill and the Sweets that in Isiolo, if a girl chews miraa with a man, it is taken for granted that she will spend the night with him. This is a bore and an embarrassment. Hassan and I are relatively friendly with each other now. We do not flirt, particularly. I have told him about the man I've left in London, several times. I've even shown him a photograph. Hassan is accustomed to mzungus. He makes it his business to befriend every one of them that comes into town. I wouldn't mind chewing miraa with him, but I am still not sure.

And I don't want to offend my Moslem neighbours. Achmed and Fauzia can hear everything that goes on. They would be appalled if they ever caught me doing it.

But Hassan is determined and I'm not, particularly. I'm also quite curious about its effect. So we chew.

★

Rich men in Isiolo chew miraa every night. Some of them chew it all day as well. Poor men chew it when they can. It is picked from bushes by women to the south of the town, in the Meru district, and brought in by the truckload every night. Isiolo is at its most alive at about ten o'clock, when the new supplies come in. More trucks go further up the road and into Somalia.

Somalia is in anarchy as I write. It was, as I sat chewing with Hassan. People are dying of starvation. There are no telephone lines. Nothing can get through to Somalia and nothing can get out (the Somali market is virtually empty. Prices for the magic material have quadrupled). Nothing can get through to Somalia, that is, except the truck loads of miraa.

The effects of miraa are a long time in coming. You chew the tops of each twig, and the bark from the end where the twig grows tougher. It tastes revolting; very bitter. So you chew it with Big D bubble gum, if you're a softie, or with a bottle of soda. The old hands take clumps of miraa between their teeth and pull. They scrape the bark clean and are left with a gob-ful, but I'm not up to that yet. Neither is Hassan.

You see the odd miraa-casualty in Isiolo, especially at night. I saw a youngish man yesterday. He was lying on the floor and shaking, jerking all over the place, sometimes mumbling, sometimes shouting to himself. The lower half of his face and his neck were smeared with green saliva. He was a casualty. He'd lost his mind. But on the whole it is a very civilised drug. You chew it for hours – four or five or more – and it keeps you awake, gives you a buzz of adrenalin, I think. It has an effect, I'd say, which is a cross between speed, coke and caffeine. It makes you believe that everything is possible; your head is filled with ideas and you don't want to go to sleep.

But miraa is no good for a Westerner in the West. It requires a great deal of patience. Until you can reach the stage where you chew without thinking, (and one reaches it fairly quickly, after a handful of evenings of genuine application) one must be willing to put in a lot of hard work. It also gives you jaw ache.

*

Anyway, Hassan and I are chewing, and I am talking neurotically about the man back home. He hands me all the juiciest, softest twigs, but I am being spoilt, can't get used to the taste. I keep spitting them out, chewing far too much gum, spitting everything out. After two hours I go on strike. The miraa is giving me a headache. It's making me sweat. (It always makes you sweat). But that's all. The endless chewing is making me feel sick and I want to go to bed.

I yawn, as a hint to Hassan, and he says he'll be moving off. He leaves me more miraa, warns me to lock all the doors and windows, says:

'You chew this, because when you are on your own you have many thoughts. Many bad thoughts.'

And he leaves. I don't want to sound sentimental, but it is the first time since I've been here that I've been treated as a human being, that I have not somehow been considered to be invincible: rich, tough, white and in the vast majority of cases, a little unwanted. Hassan, whatever Bill says, however Bill dares to treat him, regardless of the silly prices he charges Americans (and me) for a handful of bracelets, however many fatuous comments he makes about long hair, is good and imaginative and kind and I am very, very grateful to him.

*

The disco is belching its hideous Western noise across the district again tonight. Hassan asked me if I'd like to go with him the other day, but I think he knew I wouldn't. Things get pretty wild in there by all accounts. Perhaps I will go if any of my male friends come out from England. But it would be asking for trouble to go with an African, whichever African. There would be fighting.

Hassan had his Swiss watch ('And it worked') stolen from his wrist when he was there one night. 'Oh, but I was very drunk. Like this' – he shows me how he stumbled – 'very stupid.'

*

It is time, I think, to stop being so passive. To stop spending so much time lying on my bed eating mangoes and to launch an attack. So, to Achmed's place.

He is sitting in front of the television, as usual. The volume is down on the Swahili soap opera and he is nursing his radio between his legs as if it were dying, holding onto it while he listens to the World Service bulletin from London town. He is surrounded by family: brothers and children lie asleep on the bunk bed, against the walls, across the floor. He offers me a seat – the seat that Bill usually gets – and I feel honoured.

We listen to the news – crisp, middle-class accents in the middle of this nowhere – and I say to him that I am

77

ready to start teaching his children whenever he likes. The idea has been mooted before, but I've been moving around, waiting for the school to make up its mind, eating too many mangoes. And now I am tired of waiting. We can start tomorrow. I ask him if five would be convenient. He doesn't reply. Or what about half past five, I say, or six?

Half past six, he says, would be fine. I tell him I will give them five lessons a week. He nods and I wonder – have I caused offence? OK, he says, they will come round tomorrow. End of visit. Push on —

To the Ethiopian's place with the same message. He is not there, but his mother and wife are friendly enough. 'Welcome,' they say, and hand me another mango. They say I must talk to Kabede, who is at the clinic in town. I say I will go to him the following morning and push on —

To Zaidi's place to talk about the oven. She's very calm and beautiful, but she's watching television. Nothing is achieved, though of course nothing needed to be. I'm only pretending, and I head for home.

*

The same evening Hassan and I are lolling about on our own in the bungalow. There is a knock at the door. I open it.

'What?' bellows Kabede. His four children stand behind him, all carrying textbooks. 'Is nobody going to welcome us?'

'Of course,' I say, 'come on in. Karibuni.' But I can't tell if he is genuinely angry or not. He completely ignores Hassan. Hassan ignores him, wanders into the kitchen out of sight. They sit down and there are no chairs left so I sit on the floor. One of the children (all girls) offers me their seat, but I refuse.

'Leave her,' says the doctor. 'Mzungus often sit in funny places. If she wants to sit on the floor . . . Sometimes,' he laughs, 'they put up their feet like this – on the table! Ho ho.'

I tell him the arrangement. Two lessons a week for the older children. Three lessons a week for the less advanced.

'So they only get two,' he says.

'Yes. I'm not doing it at weekends.'

'Hmm.'

Six thirty is no good. Couldn't I go to the clinic? Teach them there? Seven o'clock then.

'I thought you would teach them today,' he says and he gestures irritably towards their books. I laugh, but he is annoying me again. He is not very gracious. There's no reason why I shouldn't teach them now, but Kabede is rude. I just won't.

'No. No, not today. Tomorrow.'

'Hmm.' And he leaves, his children following single-file behind him.

Have I caused offence? It certainly feels as though I have. You lose track, don't you, with these things sometimes. I am offering his children five hours of lessons for free every week, the same for Achmed's children, and I am worrying whether or not I have offended them. But I am in a very strange place, I am still a baby and I am unattractively keen to be accepted.

*

At eight I tell Hassan I have to work and he leaves, somewhat reluctantly. The whole town probably thinks

79

that we're married by now anyway, but I say goodnight to him loudly when we reach the gate in an attempt, at least, to reassure the neighbours. I think it may be too late, though. I think they think I'm a wanton woman already.

It occurs to me that they may decide I am too wanton to teach their children, and the idea keeps me awake all night.

*

I read an article in the *Nation* encouraging married women to go out for a drink occasionally with their married girlfriends. The journalist is keen to make clear that she is not advocating any form of rebellion. But the *Nation*'s ideas are so much more developed than the ones in my corner of the world. Women don't drink in Isiolo; they don't have time to drink and most of them couldn't afford it anyway. Nairobi is a world away.

Hassan says Kenyan girls are no good these days. He says they smoke and drink – but I think he's talking about the girls in the discos. I've never seen a Kenyan woman drink.

'Bah!' he says, 'no good. Not like Somali girls.'

But why, I ask, shouldn't women be allowed a share in the fun?

'Tradition.'

*

So I sit, eating mandazi and mangoes, listening to the buzz of a dying beetle, looking out for Achmed.

I was standing outside the market, talking to a man from Maralal who was promising to take me there –

80

'With my boyfriend'
'With your girlfriend, yes.'
'Boyfriend.'
'Girlfriend, yes.'
– when a big fat lorry steamed up beside me. It was blocking the progress of a mzungu car behind, which tooted impatiently. I glanced at the lorry and carried on arguing. But it was Achmed and his brother and about a thousand other people all squished up into the front. He was shouting something at me and I couldn't hear what.

'Lesson at one-thirty?' I said. He shook his head. No. 'Four-thirty?' I was grinning. It was delightful to have business to discuss.

'Postponed,' he shouted, 'until further notice.'

The noise and the Maralal man and the mzungu behind were making me flustered. I didn't ask him why. 'Postponed,' I said, still grinning. 'OK.'

I don't think I want to know why. I dread to know why. I think I have alienated the whole town now. But I have to be brave. I have to pretend that it's all OK.

*

So. It is seven o'clock. Achmed's children are no longer expected, but I am still hoping for Kabede's. I pray that they will arrive, or has the gossip reached Kabede's ears also? He saw me alone with Hassan. Perhaps he won't say anything, won't explain. He'll just stop his children from coming.

Seven-thirty passes and I am convinced. I have offended him. His children will not be coming. The whole town has turned against me and I am alone, too polluted, even, to teach their children for nothing.

I draw the curtains and begin to cook. I have reached that stage of panic where your body goes completely numb. Eight o'clock comes and I decide to eat. I play patience. Tomorrow, I tell myself, I must make plans. I must find something else to do . . .

All that silence . . .

And they arrive. The two eldest children and the mother, who leaves at once. I have never been so relieved to see anyone in my life. I ask the children to look through some text books, and they sit giggling on the sofa while I finish my food. I don't like the food, and eating it in front of them makes me very self-conscious, but they are late. And I feel I ought to make it clear that I am inconvenienced.

Grace has just arrived from Ethiopia. She can't speak a word of English and I think she is fairly thick. Esther is younger, prettier and very clever indeed.

*

Miss Kathurima's father died over the weekend, so she is not at school. She has left no message with the deputy headmistress, Mrs Tacho, whom I have met before. Mrs Tacho suggests that I try again on Wednesday, if I like. What is my name?

*

To the doctor's clinic, where I make a ghastly, pompous, patronising speech:

Of course I realise that – time – isn't exactly the same here. But when your children turned up last night, I wasn't really expecting them. Given up on them a bit. I'd started eating. So . . .'

'Yes. You know, we left here at seven on the dot, so then they got to you at seven-fourteen.'

'Well, no. They got to me after eight, so . . .'

'Yes, yes, yes.'

End of interview. Kabede is in a hurry.

*

I visit Zaidi to talk about the oven. I am expecting Bill back today, and I know he is going to Nairobi tomorrow. I suggest that, if he is willing, we should ask him to fetch the materials while he is there (we need silver paper). If not, I could take a bus to Meru next weekend. Then Zaidi says she's going to Nairobi on Thursday. She is a little put out, I think, when I suggest that she should get the materials herself.

'But I am new to Nairobi,' she says.

'Not half as new as I am.' (She doesn't seem to hear.)

'I do not even go anywhere on my own.'

She's annoying me, but she wins. I am keener to build this oven than she is, I think, to have it built. I will go to Meru on Saturday.

Back at the house I find a letter from Bill:

DAISY

WE CAME HOME. NOW WE ARE GOING TO LAKE TURKANA. SEE YOU NEXT WEEK. BILL.

Friendly lad.

I am mulling it over, thinking what revenge I can get on Bill one day, when Zulecha arrives looking very angry.

'You are cheating on me,' she says. I was supposed to visit her yesterday and the day before, but I keep forgetting. She and Maria take particular offence at the fact that they came to call when I was out.

83

'Three times, we come.'

And now I shall be missing them again. I mustn't forget to put a note on the door.

★

The doctor's children weren't late, it turns out. My clock is over an hour fast. But I'm not speaking to the neighbours, though they won't have noticed it yet, so I can't ask them the time. I must live in limbo until the fat boy comes back.

The Sweets are feeling sorry for me. They are taking me on an outing. I arrive at 6.45 a.m. for our eight o'clock meeting, and I sit on the red postbox at the bottom of the long track which leads to their house, as was arranged, watch Isiolo make its way to work and wonder at everyone's lack of punctuality.

Mr and Mrs Sweet are going to a Women's Institute charity lunch meeting at the Abberdare Country Club. Along the way we are forced to stop for the giraffes in the middle of the road. So we watch them loping and they are very beautiful.

'Aren't we lucky,' says Mrs Sweet, 'to be able to see things like that.'

Mr Sweet combs his hair as we turn through the gates of the country club.

'Aren't we lucky,' says Mrs Sweet, 'to be able to visit . . .'

This meeting proves perhaps to be the greatest culture shock of all. Booming accents straight from the pages of Agatha Christie, men with white, hairless thighs, neatly pressed khaki shorts and knee-length socks. Hard-faced women in Country Casuals talking about – what?

– handy first-aid tips, charity, how super everything is.

We climb into a bus after about half an hour of hanging around. It takes us to The Ark, another Safari Lodge. We are sat outside on a large verandah – the women put napkins on their heads to protect them from the sun – and given brunch. It is quite some feast. There is the inevitable raffle; moneys to be given to a 'charity of our choice' and we all climb back into the coach and drive home.

Mavis is coming to stay with the Sweets, so she spends most of the day with us. She's old – about sixty, say. She's written ten novels and a handful of films, but none of them has ever been published. She tells me the plot of every one. Mavis is a Catholic and she is worried, reasonably enough, about the state of my soul. She takes my address, promises to send me some of her religious poetry. Promises she'll pray that I see the light. Then she warns me about voluntary work. 'There's a woman I know,' she says, (and her face is very close) 'She was just helping an African unload some boxes in a clothes shop. And wham! Four thousand pound fine. You see the Africans – they report you. You have to be careful.'

*

I think I overdid it at the brunch. I am very, very sick. I am tossing and turning, sweating and groaning, vomiting, I fear, all over Bill's bed. My own is too far from the bathroom. And Hassan arrives.

'I am very sick,' I say, and his face lights up.

'Malaria?' He touches my forehead. 'Yes, yes. Very hot.' He leaves me, and I stumble back to the sick-stained

85

bed. I toss and turn and vomit some more. I have never been so sick. And the sound of the donkey's honk, the neighbours' television set, the cries of the children playing, bang against the walls of my foolish head, taunting me for my arrogance in ever thinking I could survive in this hell-hole, in this terrible, relentless isolation. I am frightened. I must clear up this sick before Bill comes home, but I can't move and if he doesn't come home soon God knows what will happen to me. I am obsessed by the sick, by Bill finding the sick. I must clear up this sick. It's everywhere. He mustn't see the sick on his bed.

Oh God. Perhaps I am going to die.

*

Dreaming of petty revenge against Achmed. Today I am feeling better. I hang my western knickers on the line to annoy him. Tomorrow I will sing rugby songs.

Anyway, I know I can hear it when the children come too close to the garden fence. 'Come away,' I hear, 'come away.' It's everywhere. It's in the wind.

*

The Americans won the war yesterday, but Isiolo is just the same. It's very Moslem here. In Lamu, where I travelled during the aimless weeks, they were shouting out Saddam Hussein's name along the streets. There was graffitti. But here it is just like any other day. I imagine the headlines of the *Sun*, as I sit here in this sweltering heat, and I thank God I'm not at home.

So I am sitting here with the tape recorder on, trying to do a bit of work. But the house has been invaded by

86

children. There are four of them at the moment; two of Achmed's and two that I've never seen before. Achmed's little one, Salma, she's eighteen months old, stands on her own by the door, dancing to the music. The others are playing with a ping pong ball, rather irritatingly.

Anyway, my feud with Salma's father is over, but then I don't think he ever noticed it was on. His wife came to call yesterday (I tried to hide the ashtray – she pretended not to see). She's been sick with malaria but she's better now. She said she hadn't seen me for a couple of days, wondered how I was. So I took the knickers away. I am happy again.

My neighbour's oldest boy – Hussein? Hassan? – has just come in with two delicious pieces of fudge wrapped up in brown paper. He has taken my bicycle for a ride.

It should be peculiar, perhaps. I have five Arab Moslems in the house the day after the war. Their mother is sending me fudge over the garden fence. But there is no tension. None at all.

*

Hassan has breakfast with me at the Salama. I am doing the *Nation*'s crossword – it has become quite a habit; the more you do it the easier it is. They usually have at least five clues repeated in any week – and Hassan can't help me with it. I know I will only have to pay for his mandazi and I wish he would go away. Whatever, these are small irritations and we must learn to live with them I suppose.

Then he tells me quite casually that he thinks he will go back to school. Bill's friends, the young Americans, have offered to pay his way through. If he starts next term he will have another six years before he finishes; three of them will be at the primary school. He'll have to wear shorts.

He lives well, Hassan does. Lives very free and easy. Old mzungu friends send him elegant trousers from all over the world. He has a brother in the police force who, I imagine, helps him out with a bob or two. I'm not sure about his parents. I think his father is dead, but the story changes. Sometimes he says his mother sends him money. Sometimes he says she is broke. But he doesn't want for anything. Always has plenty of miraa. Drinks at the Bomen, like Mr Sweet. Goes to the disco every Friday night.

He will have to board when he goes to school. Everybody does. Sleep in a dormitory. Probably have to share a bunk bed with three others. I'll be surprised if he sticks the six years, to be honest. But he sounds optimistic. It is brave of him even to try.

*

Hassan and I are sitting outside the house. He is chewing miraa, and has been, judging by the gabble, for quite some time. But it's peaceful enough. I don't think he really expects me to listen. The sun is going down and I am staring into space. It's nice to have company.

One of Nassir's (thirty) brothers comes around the corner. He is long and thin and old. He is wearing a long white robe and his beard is hennaed orange.

'Mzungu!' he says. He always calls me mzungu, but he always smiles, so I don't mind. 'You have friend.'

And from behind him appears a small American boy. I got to know him vaguely in Lamu, told him (I assume) that if he was passing this way he should come and call. But now he is here, looking small and shy and apologetic and I can't remember his name. Hassan gabbles over the silence which should have been filled with some sort of introduction. He gabbles for the rest of the evening. We go to the Salama (a hoteli which belongs to Nassir's brother with the red beard) for a bit of camel meat and Hassan gabbles throughout. It's a bit of a relief actually. He's a nice boy, Douglas, but it turns out he is a little dull.

In the morning I take him for a walk around the town. We can't use Bill's bike, of course, because he's locked it up. They are roasting goats' heads behind the market place. Douglas says:

'Oh boy! Are you going to eat that?'

'Very nice,' says the roaster. 'Put onions and tomatoes . . .' We move away.

*

We bump into Peter and Japan, an elderly bangle boy whom I last saw eating bananas at the Isiolo hotel. One of their colleagues, a Somali boy of nineteen, is getting married this afternoon. Would we like to come?

We are led through the market and way beyond, up dirt tracks, past grass huts overflowing with children. Finally, we come to the bride's mother's house. More children are hanging around. They are singing; making a peculiar, high-pitched sound, anyway. The noise, we are told, is meant to signify a wedding.

The bride is nowhere to be seen. Her mother stands at the giko behind a delapidated hut. She is cooking an enormous curry. We are presented, made very welcome, led into the hut, given plates and knives and stools to sit on. The nine other guests – all male, all, except Japan, under the age of twenty-five, sit down on the floor.

The walls of the hut are made from uncut milk cartons. Its ceilings, from empty sacks of sugar. And we are given orange juice and a separate bowl of curry; delicious curry, but there's enough there to feed us forever.

The lunch is over and so, for the moment, are the celebrations. This evening there will be dancing, we are told. We must come back later.

It is arranged that Douglas will go to the dancing alone. I am supposed to go with Maria (of the Zulecha duo) to visit her sister, who is studying at the secretarial college a mile or two up the road. Maria is offended by me for various reasons: I have skipped too many of our meetings. And I daren't duck out. I'm also supposed to be giving a lesson to the Ethiopians. But I'm so angry with bloody Kabede I want to put a stop to the whole arrangement. I keep nearly doing it, but then his children and his wife and his mother are so very nice. Most of his children are so clever it's a pleasure to teach them. Whatever. The latest outrage:

I was talking to some people called Nancy and Monica under the fruit-selling tree. Kabede turns up, interrupts the conversation, doesn't even say hello, takes a hold of my bicycle, says, 'I want it', and rides it away.

'Don't take it for long,' I say as he goes. He looks ridiculous anyway. He's far too big for it. He turns around (still peddling) says, 'No, I take it to the police station', which is miles away. So I laugh. I don't believe him. Carry on with the Swahili lesson under the tree. And I wait. And wait. But he doesn't return.

Eventually I walk home, think perhaps he might have left it for me there. No. I return to the tree. No bicycle. So I go to his house, leaving poisonous messages for him with everyone I meet in between. His wife doesn't know where it is. She says perhaps he has gone to the police station. And she takes me there. (I find out later that she is suffering from a bout of malaria, but she doesn't say anything then. And I'm so annoyed, I'm unlikely to notice it on my own.)

I find the bike. It's resting outside the bloody police station as if it were the most natural place in the world. But this is nearly an hour later. And on top of that, bear in mind, I discovered yesterday that the bastard had tried to buy the bike off the Sweets for one of his daughters. Without telling me.

Well, I bump into him in town later on in the day. 'Oh ho, Kabede,' I say. I'm trying to be good humoured. 'You took my bicycle away.' And then HE is angry with ME because he had to come back from the police station on foot. God, I hate him. Even then, he could barely look at me, spare half a second to discuss when to make up for the lesson I had cancelled, in celebration of the arrival of my small American friend.

All very annoying, I'm sure you agree. So Douglas goes off for the dancing and I meet up with him in the market place later on. We find each other. He's wandering around, looking a little lost, a little dull, I'm afraid. He says the dancing never happened. But we're supposed to go back to the Isiolo hotel. There should be a matatu waiting for us there.

A matatu indeed. And there is. We do a little more hanging around and then the driver and owner of the bus (he's a smooth, relatively sophisticated Indian boy whose father owns the largest shop in the town. I never do get his name, though we become vague friends, eventually) takes us off to another hut. This one belongs to the groom. Its walls are made from brown parcel paper and so is its ceiling. Bits of string hang off the walls in some attempt, I think, at festive decoration.

A row of twelve brightly-coloured women are singing a welcome to us all. But within minutes of our arrival one of them comes into the hut. They are tired. The Indian boy gives them a lift home.

On the bed there sit two girls. One, the thinner, younger looking of the two is introduced as the bride. She is in ordinary Somali clothing. She keeps a veil over her face, and her face turned to the wall. She says nothing. Neither does her friend. But at least her friend only looks bored. The bride looks painfully shy. She looks miserable. I try to talk to her, in my pathetic Swahili. I try a couple of times. But each time I do, the boys fall silent and the bride looks as though she might be about to cry. She doesn't understand my Swahili. I can't hear her replies. I give up. We are getting nowhere.

So the poor Somali girls push themselves a little further back towards the wall. The rest of us sit around the lantern, make desultory conversation about nothing, sometimes in English, sometimes in Swahili. We listen to Bros on a cranky tape machine. The boys chew. We all drink sodas. And nothing happens. The bride is ignored.

That's the party. It's over. But there is something odd going on. Where are all the old people? Why does everyone look so sad?

Peter tells Douglas that the reason festivities are so low-key is because the bride already has a daughter. At which point why did they have all the singing, why the curry? Why were Douglas and I asked to come along? I don't understand. I don't understand it at all.

★

It has been arranged that Maria (of the Zulecha duo again) and Monica, the fat young daughter of one of the women who lies under the fruit-selling tree, are to come around this afternoon and teach me how to cook mandazi.

Maria takes me shopping, makes me buy far too much. Mandazi is supposed to be a poor man's food (lumps of dough mixed with spices, cut into triangles and deep fried). They only cost 2ksh (4p) in the hotelis, but she somehow manages to bring the ingredients' cost up to £5. It usually takes me a week to spend £5 in Isiolo.

We spend hours in the kitchen. Monica and Maria both appear to be very confident, but they keep adding more oil to the mixture, then more sugar. They've put a whole bottle of oil in now. I don't know what's going on.

They leave, finally. And I have a hundred mandazi to get through on my own. They're disgusting. Absolutely disgusting. I try to palm a few off on Hassan, but he tastes one of them and laughs. It takes a while, but eventually even the look of them makes me want to throw up. I chuck them away. Make a note never to take a cooking lesson from the overweight teenagers again.

*

Nassir comes a-rattling at the gate. Bill isn't around. It's night time, so I don't ask him in. He stands on the other side of the padlocked gate and we discuss my teaching prospects. He says his sister is a headmistress in Wajir (further north. It's very hot in Wajir). He says she is 'an influential woman'. He is sure she will be able to give me a job. I believe him. It's good to have a back up plan.

Mzungu breakfast at the Bomen. It's overpriced and fairly nasty, but it doesn't matter. It's still a treat.

A large white man with a red face comes striding into the bar. He is holding a 200ksh note – an absurdly anti-social offering for Isiolo. Nobody deals in 200ksh notes.

'You run a business,' he bellows at the waiter, 'and you don't have any change? Whassamatter with you?'

He makes me ashamed.

I meet a man called Bernard who seems to know the whole of the London Underground map by heart. It would be impossible to describe the pleasure I draw from reminiscing over which comes first on the Metropolitan line, Westbourne Park or Baker Street.

★

The doctor comes around to pick up his children after their evening lesson. I try to keep on hating him, but he is very charming. And he has invited me to dinner tomorrow evening, so I love him now, after all.

We don't talk much during the dinner. We sit in silence watching television. But the food is delicious and I don't really mind. It's a pleasure, surprisingly, to spend an evening with a family. They are so cosy and ordinary together, and the youngest child whines, and the oldest child tells her to shut up. I am quite settled in, quite comfortable. But then Kabede asks me when I'm planning to go home. He wants to watch the rest of the television programmes on his own.

★

Back to school. Still no Kathurima. 'I should give up,' says Mrs Tacho, but I won't. Seileesh says he will have a word with the mayor. Of course he won't.

*

Achmed returns from a long-haul trip to Wajir. His wife has recovered from another bout of malaria but now she is in bed suffering from burns. She poured a saucepan full of boiling mandazi oil onto her arm yesterday. She's treating it with a horrible looking home-brewed medicine which she keeps in an old soda bottle and it's making Bill very uptight. He tells her she should go to the hospital and use Western treatments but she refuses. He thinks she's stupid. He's so angry, Bill. He's always so angry – and so rude. I don't think this country is doing him any good at all. The people are too polite to him. He gets away with murder.

Anyway, Achmed offers me a sweet pink milky drink and asks if I'd mind teaching his children on Saturdays.

*

Henry, the lazy watchman, has gone off with my bicycle again. Where is he? He's never around except when he's after a smoke. When Bill's away he disappears completely.

*

Zulecha and Maria come around again. I'm not very hospitable, but I can't help it. They irritate me. I can't see where our friendship could possibly be leading. I talk about the novel I'm writing, although I know they're not interested. I ask them if it's just the Boran women who

95

are so very shy with men.

And they giggle.

'What do you think, then, when you see me, not being shy with men?'

'Nothing.' (In unison. Too fast).

'No. Too fast. That's not the truth.'

'If Boran woman is not shy with man we think she is . . . prostitute.'

'ZULECHA!' says Maria.

And they giggle again.

*

There's a man at the post office I haven't mentioned before. He's called Joseph and he's an awful creep. When he sees me in the queue he pushes everyone aside so he can serve me, leans right over the counter and asks, with a terrible grin:

'And how is the day? Ye-es, ye-es. And when are you having lunch with me?'

I am waiting there, in a small room with a telephone, because I am expecting a call from home. It doesn't come but I wait all the same. It's a pleasant room. Joseph comes in, sits far too close to me, says he wants to 'do some chatting. Ye-es', asks:

'So. How was the Gulf War? I enjoyed it thoroughly.'

I say I didn't.

'But I wanted Saddam to be beaten and punished.' He's only saying it to suck up, so I am very cold. I decide to give up on the call from home, try to put one through to London instead.

Joseph talks to the operator:

'Ye-es. A mzungu wants to make a reverse charge

call to London, England. Is it possible? The women they concentrate on their work in your country,' he says, as we hang on . . . and on. 'But ours, they justie chatter. Ye-es, huh huh, ye-es.'

Oh, but I want to hit him. And I never did get through.

*

Miss Kathurima has returned. I am to start teaching tomorrow. Twelve lessons a week, then. And no grammar, only composition.

'But will that work?' says the English teacher. 'Who will teach them their grammar?'

'She'll only be here until the end of June – or, at the very latest, the end of July.'

Twelve lessons doesn't sound like much. But it's very hot out here. I've grown quite accustomed to my afternoon nap. And by now I am fairly obsessed with my novel. Things couldn't be better. I couldn't ask for more.

Nancy has returned to her place under the fruit-selling tree. She tells me that she's been sick, that she has been missing me very much.

'*Very* much?' I say and I laugh, and so does she, but I don't know if she understands why. She says she's had malaria. I'm beginning to wonder if 'malaria' isn't just another word for illness.

*

A camp old man who sits out on the main street with a sewing machine is making me a teacher's dress; a more modest something to be fit for the classroom. I've known him for a while now. He teaches me Swahili, asks me when I'm going to give him some business, holds three hundred conversations at once, shouts at the passing children for making noises which he thinks may be annoying me.

'What is the matter with you?' he shouts after them, but they ignore him and he never waits for a reply.

*

So. There are ninety-five pupils, all of whom are taller than I am, in my class today. Half the first form, aged fifteen to eighteen, have yet to turn up, though the end of term is only five weeks away. The rest are waiting for a document to be signed so they can use the other classroom. They squash up on the thirty desks and various benches and are remarkably co-operative, all things considered – considering, especially, that I clearly don't have an idea what I'm supposed to be doing. The only solid piece of advice I've been given is to avoid teaching literature that mentions the winter. The winter is of little interest, apparently, to people in Isiolo.

A bell goes for the end of the lesson, and I say OK, I'll be off then. But they call me back. They say 'Stay, Madam, stay. We don't have a timetable.' And I'm very flattered, so I stay, but I've run out of things to talk about.

*

I call in on Fauzia. She is looking pale and ill and her burn is horrible. She says tomorrow she will teach me how to cook 'goody-goodies', (the fudge that her son brought round the other day). I tell her about my new dress. I've picked it up from the camp dressmaker and it's very large – but that doesn't matter. It's also completely transparent. Isn't it funny, Fauzia, I say, when I got it especially because I needed something to make me look decent.

Ho ho. We have a laugh and some chai and some delicious mandazi and I leave her alone.

A couple of minutes later she is shouting at me to come out to the garden fence. She has two petticoats and a bra in her hand. Oh, I'm very embarrassed, pretend not to notice the bra, take one of the petticoats, say thanks and run back into the house. She returns later on in the afternoon. Now she's carrying three bras. I can try them all on for size and . . . Oooooh! This is the most embarrassing moment of my life. Never mind. Asante sana. And of course she's saved me some money. I will give everything back to her at the end of my stay. In the meantime it means I can wear this wretched, ugly dress without offending anybody.

*

I have seven children at my evening class today. Three of Achmed's (two of whom have brought their maths) and four Ethiopians. I think I'm going to have to split them up. I don't have time to explain anything to any of them.

Fauzia invites me to dinner after the lesson. Liverpool v someone on the box. Achmed comes back late from a trip to Meru. He brings crayons for the children, currants and ice-cream and pineapple for his wife. Fauzia gives the pineapple to me.

*

'No. You're two sentences behind. Can you listen, please. There's no point in doing this if you're not going to listen.' But she is. It's me who isn't. Form 1's lessons go only fairly well. The students are very polite.

The classroom for 1E still hasn't been passed 'by the council for . . . council for building, I think' according to the elderly Swahili teacher. He says it will happen this weekend. They're supposed to be passing the new dormitory at the same time. At the moment students are sleeping two or three to a bed. But I am learning a little about Isiolo now. I should be surprised if the council comes anywhere near the school before the end of the bloody century.

*

It is Woman's Day in Kenya today. I read an article in the *Nation* which complains that Woman's Day is meaningless in a country where the women have neither the time nor the money to celebrate.

In Isiolo there is very little money but still the football pitch off the main street has been taken over by tribal dances for the occasion. Mama Fatima, Zulecha's mother, acts as compère. Isiolo Girls has been given the afternoon off lessons to go and watch. The DC and the new DO will both be making speeches.

'Somali women dancing is best,' says Hassan. I don't tell him in case it hurts his feelings, and the Somalis aren't bad at all, but they're not the best. It's the Turkana who really get the house going. They sing a song celebrating the progress of women's freedom and they throw their wiry bodies and angry faces high up into the air, and they make a terrifying sight.

But then they seem to get a bit carried away. They refuse to stop. The DC is standing up, making signs that he wants to speak. Still, they keep on dancing and chanting. Eventually the police have to chase them off the field.

*

There are two other white girls on the football pitch and I am curious to know who they are. Hassan doesn't know, but I imagine he won't take long to find out. One of them wears a mini skirt. She is smoking. I think, 'Well, *really*!' She sticks out like a sore thumb.

*

Fauzia is sitting on the step outside her living room door, peeling the skins off a bucketful of rock-hard mangoes. She calls me over and I join her. The children hang around, on the look out for any mangoes she decides are over ripe. She sends her daughter to fetch another knife and we peel the rest of them together. We watch the sun go down. I am very happy. This evening she will teach me to cook mandazi.

Fauzia breaks off mango-peeling at various points in order to go away and pray. She's often doing that, actually – in the middle of a conversation, whatever – but she does it without even a hint of self-consciousness, as if it were the most natural thing in the world.

Ramadan is drawing nearer. Fauzia mentions it three

or four times a day. She's looking forward to it, keeps asking me if I'll be willing to join in. I laugh, say maybe, perhaps, I'll let you know. And I'm considering it. I like to think that I may.

*

I'll tell you quickly here how to cook a Swahili breakfast (mandazi and chai). If recipes bore you, jump on to the next asterisk. These are the only ones:

MANDAZI:

To make the dough: 1/2 kg plain flour, 1 tablespoon of margarine, ground up seeds of 2–3 cardamom pods, 1/4 cup sugar, 1/4 teaspoon dissolved yeast, milk.

Knead. Divide into five smaller lumps and knead again. Knead into five small balls. Leave on a plate and under a saucepan overnight. (NB: remember the balls will expand.)

Some four to seven hours later: roll into circles. Cut circles into quarters. Deep fry.

The oil needs to get used to the mandazi, so the first few won't work. Cut one or two of the triangles into little pieces and leave them until they're dark brown. Throw them away. Put whole triangles in and watch them puff up dramatically. Leave for only a short time, until golden. Then eat.

CHAI:

Pour equal amounts of water and milk into saucepan. Add dessert spoon of freshly ground cinnamon, ginger, cardamom. Add tea leaves and more sugar than you'll think you want. Leave to simmer. Drain. Drink with mandazi.

*

It was decided that I should teach Maria and Hussein, the two more intelligent of Fauzia's children, only twice a week. Hassan, the eldest – he's fourteen – would be taught every night at the same time as the Ethiopians. Hassan is very lazy and he doesn't know how to read.

Since then my evening classes have turned into some sort of adolescent dating agency. Nobody will pay any attention to me at all. My students spend the whole time flirting, and they won't even do it in English! Never mind. The Ethiopian girls are worked very hard already. They have extra lessons with the neat primary school teacher even before they get to me. They have extra lessons at the weekends with him, too. Classes at school begin at eight. They study right through the day without a break and they don't usually leave me until quarter to nine in the evening. It seems a shame about Hassan, though, because he's perfectly intelligent. I should talk to his parents I suppose, but they're so laid back. They don't seem able to do much about him either.

'Hassan gives me a headache,' says Fauzia later. 'He will not go to school. He will not go to Madrassa. When his father is away he does what he likes.'

Which includes taking my bicycle away for half an hour and bringing it back, totally bashed up, a fortnight later.

'Well, I thought,' says Bill, when I meet him one day in the street, 'you shouldn't be lending that bike to Hassan. It's not even yours.' He shrugs, smirks, limps off into the dust.

Nassir brings a friend around with him who is just back from meeting his future wife's parents in Nairobi.

'And now they will elope,' says Nassir. He talks quickly; he's always very matter of fact. His friend doesn't seem to speak English. The groom's brother or a good friend, he explains, will go to the in-laws after the wedding. They will offer the parents 500ksh, apologise for any inconvenience and that will be the end of that.

'Otherwise, the father isn't there or the brother isn't there – and the parents want celebrations. It can get very expensive. Maybe delayed for two or three years. No problem. Lots of people do it.'

★

The American ambassador will be stopping off in Isiolo on his way back from the North. Bill is in a bit of a dither.

Achmed says: 'I will kill him. I'll put a poster of Saddam Hussein on the wall. I'll refuse to let him into the house.'

Bill says: 'But I said he could come round here and chew miraa.'

And they laugh.

★

Back from Meru with a cardboard box and a packet of silver paper. Everyone wants to know where I have gone and, more importantly, what I'm carrying in the box. A few people just take it off my shoulders and open it – are generally disappointed by what's inside. This is the first time, perhaps, as I walk through the town with my stupid box, fresh off the bus from Meru, that I feel I am home in Isiolo. It's the box that makes people greet me so warmly. But still. They greet me. And I know them – their names, their faces, a tiny bit about their lives. I love Isiolo this evening; far, far more than I ever loved Ladbroke Grove.

I am walking past a shop that sells very good honey. A fat old woman comes out.

'Sst! We! Mzungu!'

She leads me to the back room, brings with her a man who can speak English. I am wearing a very decent cotton skirt. It reaches my ankles. But she points to her petticoats. The translator says:

'The lady wants you to wear a petticoat. Otherwise it's as if you are walking around the town NAKED!'

Too bad.

Wanjella is walking with a young child. He invites me to dinner the following night and I accept because I assume that the child is one of his.

Lucy, of the post office and the yellow accessories, (today is a pink day) grabs me around the waist again, and I am defenceless because I'm carrying the cardboard box. I tell her I'll be cooking mandazi tomorrow. She says, with the head thrown back, the ridiculous laugh:

'You're not serious!' And she asks me back to her place for tea. 'It's very small, my home,' she says, over and over again as I follow behind, trying to fit the cardboard box through the measly corridor which leads to her room.

And it is. The size of a large kitchen table. A grubby white cotton curtain divides the single bed from the two stools and the giko, crushed up beside the door. On the walls are photographs of her three children (away at boarding school) and her husband, who is working in

Nairobi. She offers me a banana, and we sit on the stools, and our knees bump. She has been waiting for a transfer to Nairobi for nearly a year. In the meantime, this is her life, her home. And the greedy look in her eye, the phoney, flirtatious manner, are suddenly much easier to ignore.

'I love Isiolo.' As I do, this evening.

'Haaa. You're not serious?' And we say goodbye.

*

I go to Hassan's place – or to the courtyard outside it – to pick up some miraa. I refuse to come in. It would be asking for trouble (rumours, not Hassan), and he pretends not to understand why. Two women lie on the ground outside the cubicle next door to his. They are clearly prostitutes, they have the hard, world-weary look in their eyes and they are chewing. One of them tosses her Big D wrapper into the air and it lands on the other one's bottom. The other one turns soon after it lands, looks at it, leaves it there.

*

Hassan has discovered who the white girls in mini skirts are. Daughters of a Dutch volunteer who Bill sometimes talks about, but whom I've never met. Peter and a friend of his took them to the disco last night. They all got very drunk. One of the girls danced with somebody else. There was a fight. Hassan offered 20 ksh to the newcomer, on condition he leave both girls alone.

'Oh,' says Hassan, 'very stupid girls. They are drunk – like this!' He mimes another stumble. 'Very stupid boys!' and he flicks his elegant, Somali wrist with disdain. 'Without me it would have been war. I don't like those girls.

106

No. I don't want them.'

*

I am having a certain amount of trouble keeping my class under control. But at least they talk in English when they talk amongst themselves.

Big green oranges have come to town. And so have the rains. You can't really teach during the rains. The noise on the corrugated roof is deafening. Everything has to be done on the board.

I am sitting in the staff room. The old Swahili teacher is teasing the young science teacher, who is resting his head on his desk and complaining that he is bored.

'He thinks,' says the old man to anybody who will listen, 'because he has feathers on his face that he is old . . .'

'I don't know why you have to go on about age,' says the science teacher. 'And now I have no lessons today. I am very bored.'

So why doesn't he go home?

'But I am bored at home. I only sleep.'

*

I walk past a rubbish heap on my way to school and from it, perfectly camouflaged, I would never have seen him, jumps a poor boy with skinny legs. He is part of the rubbish, this skinny boy. I give him some rubbishy change.

And move on . . .

*

Nassir has taken to calling me mwalimu. I like that. He is here today, for lack of anything else to do; he's sitting outside while I give my evening class. Kabede's wife arrives early to take the children away. I offer her a seat beside Nassir, and an orange and wonder, twenty minutes on, at how slowly she is eating it. She has cut it into four pieces and is still fussing about with the first. The lesson ends. She hands the rest of the orange to her children.

★

Dinner with Wanjella. He has no family. He has the dirtiest cubicle I have ever seen. It's about three times the size of Lucy's place; it even has electricity, which is rare enough. But I've never seen anywhere so cluttered with dirty nonsense. It is an unpleasant place to be.

Wanjella sits, then lies, on his filthy, crumpled double bed. He is angry with the West, with white people. But at the same time he is greedy for everything that he's decided a white person may have to offer. So ours is an uncomfortable relationship and I am not comfortable there. I perch on the edge of my stool and listen to the rustling sounds coming from somewhere behind the paraffin giko. Wanjella is cooking me maize, if he can ever find it underneath all those dirty clothes, broken dreams, bits of paper, rotting pieces of junk.

He says, as he lies there and I look out for the cause of the noise, that Western women don't worry about their appearance in the same way that African women do. He doesn't want to marry a Kenyan woman. She'll make him spend all his money on her clothes. I tell him he's wrong. Western women are often extremely interested in clothes, but he won't listen. Instead he corrects my English grammar, which is rather annoying, because he's wrong about that, too.

But there's the rustle again – and it's so disgusting in here. This time whatever it is that's causing it nearly knocks the maize pot off the giko, and I feel it's reasonable enough to make a comment —

'What?' he says. 'Oh,' and lies back on the dirty bed not in the least disturbed. Suddenly from beneath the rubble jumps an enormous toad. Well, that's a relief. Could have been something far worse.

Wanjella has many problems. He shows me photographs of what he claims to be his father's country house. It's enormous. He says that his family is rich, that they have paid for his brother to be educated in India and for his sister to go to Canada, where she has now settled down. But he says that when it was his turn to go to university, his father suddenly decided he was tired of funding his children. Wanjella must pay his own way through.

So then, I ask, why can't one of his siblings help him out? But no. 'They have Western ideas now.' He says he is in Isiolo which he hates (he's been here for almost three years), because it's easier to get some kind of university scholarship if you apply from an arid area. I don't know whether to believe his stories. But I don't like his dirty cubicle or the ridiculous way he is lounging on his bed. And I want to go home.

*

My class won't stop talking. The students are giving me a sore throat. All the other classes are so quiet. I had to send someone out today, just to show the others that

I meant what I said. But it made no difference to them at all.

Later on I persuade them, row by row, to recite the following poem:

> A girl who weighed more than an ounce
> Used language I dare not pronounce.
> When a man, so unkind,
> Pulled her chair from behind,
> To see, so he said, if she'd bounce.

It turns into a competition, because the back row is so feeble, and I am clearly so pleased when the third row recites it better. By the time we get to the front they are bawling it out. You could have heard them all the way through the district. It is quite funny, but then everyone gets over excited and I lose control again.

I spend the next hour trying to explain what the poem is about. I take the only chair in the room (everyone sits on benches) to illustrate the pulling away point. And the only chair in the room is being sat on by the only fat girl in the school. I don't know, but she doesn't seem to mind.

Just as the bell goes the class gets the poem's joke. As I leave they are roaring with laughter.

It would be a shame after this long wait if the head-mistress has to ask me to stop teaching. Unless my students quieten down I fear that may well be what happens.

*

Hassan is driving me mad. I am sitting at home trying to work. He says, 'All these words, Daisy. Now you are tired.' I ignore him. He is sitting opposite me holding a piece of cardboard. And he bites it.

'Look,' he says, 'I cut.'

I ignore him. He puts his arm between his teeth and pretends to bite.

'Look. Daisy. I cut me.'

I ignore him.

'Ahh, Hassan,' he says, 'why you cut me?'

I ignore him.

'Look. Daisy.' He goes through the whole bloody rigmarole again.

*

One of the teachers, she's small and she's always angry, comes storming into the staff room.

'I will NOT teach that class again. They annoy me.'

'Why?' asks the elderly Swahili teacher in ever such a gentle voice.

A girl who was short of a desk had taken the teacher's desk and put the books that were resting on it onto the floor.

'That class. They annoy me. I WILL NOT teach them again.'

But there are only six classes in the school . . . Can she really be allowed just to refuse to teach one of them? These teachers are out of control. They don't like me much, either.

*

Fauzia's wound has cleared up completely. She gives me chai and chapati with honey and talks about Ramadan. It begins in a few days' time. Nobody knows on exactly what day, of course, because it depends on when they first see the new moon. Fauzia points to a star – it may be the Northern star – 'When it shines alone,' she says, which it does now, 'a new moon will come very soon.' She is looking forward to Ramadan. She is still trying to persuade Bill and me to join her in it. And maybe I will. Her holiness is quite inspiring.

Bill turns up with a toothy Somali girl. I assume they are lovers, because he hasn't been around for a couple of days and the pair of them are chewing.

'Tst,' says Fauzia, as she watches them walk away, but she says it terribly gently, 'Willy thinks he's very good.'

*

Henry, the idle watchman, has been doing a bit of work. He was burning a pile of rubbish this afternoon and he somehow managed to set fire to a bees' nest at the same time. Now his arm has swollen up like a football, but he seems to be OK.

*

A staff meeting has been called at the school this morning. It is supposed to happen at eight but it doesn't begin until after ten. Only half the teachers bother to turn up. Miss Kathurima is not among them. She left for Meru several weeks ago. Mrs Tacho, I learn finally, is the new head-mistress.

Items discussed include:

1. The setting of exams.
2. The name of the new dormitory (discussed at length).
3. Arrangements for the open day. It was supposed to have taken place some time in April, but things have been left too late now. It will probably happen in July.
4. The growing trend, amongst students, for wearing non-identical navy blue skirts.
5. The whereabouts of the new basketball court, promised, one assumes, in moments of wild optimism, by the last two headmistresses.
6. The distribution of fifty new desks which arrived today.

At this point the staff suddenly become quite animated. Up until now they have been sulky, barely able to raise their heads from their desks with the trouble of it all. Mrs Tacho is clearly relieved that she has finally attracted their attention. I gather that relations between her and her staff are not what they ought to be. She is an Indian. Anyway, the angry woman (who has refused to teach one of the classes) gets very angry indeed at the suggestion that the desks should be given to 2E. Each class is considered. If 1W gets all the new desks then 1W will think that it is better than 1E. But 1W made a greater contribution towards the new desk fund . . . It's decided, finally, that the desks should be divided between both the first year classes.

Meanwhile the school hasn't received any money from the government since July. Students are being turned away because they can't come up with the fees. Last term's food bill has yet to be paid. The new dormitory is not allowed by the health people to be opened until it has seven new lavatories, but the school doesn't have the money for seven lavatories or anywhere near. And the teachers are worrying about bloody basketball, non-identical blue skirts. Astonishing, isn't it, how similarly fatuous people are all over the world.

Anyway, I am very sensible. I know that I am resented here. I know that it's only because I've been so pushy that they've allowed me to get in at all. Obviously, I don't say a word. About anything. I have nothing to say.

At assembly the following morning Mrs Tacho tells the students of a new school rule. Too many students, she says, have been getting off sick and then spending the day walking across town, meandering to the Isiolo hospital.

'I will refuse permission for children to go to hospital on Tuesdays, Fridays, Saturdays and Sundays,' she whispers from her superior position in the long, hot grass, 'unless it is essential. No permission will be given for a common cold or a boil.'

Assembly dismissed. But there are rumblings, I gather, of discontent. Mrs Tacho is no more popular with her students than she is with her staff.

*

Another of Fauzia's sisters has turned up. She came to call on me, with her four children, only seconds after she watched Hassan (junior) come over for his nightly flirting session with the Ethiopians. She sat, smiling, but she wouldn't take any tea and the students seemed to find her rather a distraction from their mating games. Anyway, odd thing is she's a new sister, younger than the other two, but her children are exactly the same.

Esther, the cleverest of the Ethiopian children, is giving a talk to the rest of the children in English about why she thinks school uniform is a bad idea. Hassan is supposed to oppose the motion, but he refuses; says he wants to play I Spy.

'School uniform bad because – nini – (tee hee) – you, Moulu – shut you, tee hee. Nini . . .'

Is bad. School uniform *is* bad. Come on, Esther. Stop fooling around. Get on with it.

'But no I cannot, nini. Hassan he annoying me, tee hee hee.'

Come ON!

'School uniform, he is bad because erm, nini, my Daddy he rich and I have many beautiful clothe and I want everyone is seeing I am rich.'

*

I had been planning to stop at the Salama for breakfast but Peter and Hassan are outside, lolling about, asking questions about my movements, ready to drop nothing to join in. So I tell them I am going for a bicycle ride.

Which I do.

Half a mile later I find a goat lying in the middle of the road. It is blocking my progress and half its belly is hanging out. I wonder as I draw closer if it is dead. But from behind it staggers a very little one, born, I discover from its owner (through mime, not words), about thirty seconds before I arrived. Our conversation – and both of us are grinning, with all the good will in the world – goes like this:

D: 'Ii ni kidogo sana.' It is very small.

G.O: 'Aya. Aya.' Yes, that's right.

D: 'Kidogo kidogo.' Very very small.

G.O: 'Aya. Kidogo sana.' Yes. Very small.

D: 'Mzuri mzuri. Mzuri sana, kidogo.' Very very good. Very good, little.

G.O: 'Aya. Mzuri sana.' Yes. Very good.

D: 'Kwa heri mzee.' Goodbye, old sir.

G.O: 'Aya, mzungu. Kwaheri.' Yes, white. Goodbye.

*

I have been invited to a staff room lunch. It is supposed to start at one, but I am learning. Turn up at twenty past and the school is deserted. The staff room door is locked. I sit on the step outside and listen to the sound of the gushing tap. But nobody comes. Quarter to two and I give up.

A friend of mine from England is expected here within the next couple of days. She might arrive on the afternoon bus from Nairobi. Nothing else to do. I hang around at the bus station though the bus isn't due for at least another hour and eat another seven mandazi. Desultory conversation with passers by – they all know I am expecting a friend. They have been asking me when she is coming for weeks. Some people are pleased for me, I think. They say I am often looking lonely.

I don't feel it, though, these days. Hardly at all.

The bus is late. I am filled with mandazi and tired of waiting. It's unlikely that she will be here today. I return home.

*

Mr Job is sitting on the tree that Henry sits on occasionally – it's the watchman's post. He says he's been waiting for me. I had forgotten he was supposed to come round.

When he's not making jewellery, Mr Job is an electrician. He needs to get into our bungalow in order to disguise the wires which run over the garden fence to Achmed's place. Our neighbours are waiting for a spare part . . .

. . . In the meantime they must take the electricity from Bill. Something like that. Anyway, it's illegal which is why the wires have to be disguised. Mr Job is complaining about Achmed – 'he's like an African. Now he says I must get the spare part when he has money, and time is money' – when Peter arrives.

Peter tells me that there were no mzungus on the Nairobi bus this afternoon. He hangs around. There is another bus due in later.

Laura turns out to be on it. So Mr Job and Peter hang around a bit more. Achmed comes to call with a cupful of toffee-flavoured jelly. It's a welcoming present to Laura from his wife. Hassan turns up with a couple of joints, rolled from the pages of the *Daily Nation*. They're a welcoming present ordered ages ago in great expectation from me. The grass is incredibly strong out here. I slip the joints into my back pocket and wait and we all do an awful lot more of nothing.

*

Hours later and the curtains have been drawn in a fairly hopeless attempt to disguise the sound of mzungu girls' drug induced laughter. I don't want Achmed and Fauzia having any idea what I'm up to. The dawn is breaking as Laura says:

'What is the point of all this solid, solid living?'

And I say:

'Your life is living.'

And we write it down, think all our problems have been solved and go to bed.

*

Peter turns up at nine this morning with a creepy man called Mohammed who can't stop talking. Mohammed, a primary school teacher with a shady past – something to do with ivory, I suspect – has a Land Rover. He says he will rent it to us for $100 a day.

Well neither of us can possibly afford that, not even for a quarter of a day, so he leaves, chattering and gabbling about what a bargain we're missing, about the recent deterioration of his health, about anything, anywhere. Nothing. But he must leave. This morning I have the first hangover since leaving Ladbroke Grove.

*

There has been a feeling of expectation in Isiolo for several weeks now, a muffled buzz, as the world anticipates Ramadan. And this evening, as the sun is setting orange over the enormous sky, shining through the empty windows of empty building sites, lending beauty to the piles of rubble, to the skinny, sore-ridden donkey ambling by, most of Fauzia's family is standing in a huddle at their kitchen door. They are looking up into the orange sky. The men – Achmed, his two brothers, one of Seileesh's builders – stand, outlined, on the cabin of the monstrous lorry. They are looking up, calling out, pointing into the orange sky. And up there, somewhere, a Christian would never have noticed it, is a tiny speck. The new moon is shining.

Seileesh's builder is having his final daylight chew. 'It's very good,' he says (in Swahili), 'when you chew, you look at his house and you think it's yours.' Henry, a Christian of course, is struggling like the rest of us to see what all the fuss is about. He's up there on the lorry too. Everyone is pointing towards stars and clouds and in between, but —

'No. I cantie see it. Itees above the clouddie. You are youngy. You shouldie see itty, ho ho.' And he climbs back down to his post, chuckling.

Isiolo will celebrate tonight. Tomorrow the fasting begins. Again, Fauzia asks if Bill and I will be joining her in it.

Again, I say perhaps, and every time I say perhaps I almost believe that I will.

All the best hotelis will be closed for Ramadan anyway, so perhaps I shall be forced to.

*

Bill has turned Laura and me out of the house this evening because he thinks he may be going to get laid. We decide to make the long walk up to Save the Elephant Restaurant where you can often get chicken. But it is a slow business.

We bump into the science teacher (of the feathery face) who insists that we stop off at his house along the way. He offers us bananas and asks me yet again, just as he asks me every time he sees me, if I will leave him my Walkman when I go back home. I always say no. I don't like him much. And the three of us have very little to say to each other. We sit in his house – it's spacious and very bare. Teachers posted to Isiolo tend to live relatively well. They are given a hardship allowance by the government because nobody wants to come here. They have little to spend the allowance on because Isiolo is not a consumer's haven, it's a hardship area. So the money is spent on miraa.

The only luxury item in his big, bare sitting room is an old paperback, a cowboy book, whose cover is so worn that its title is impossible to decipher. There are Christian pictures on the walls. Little else.

He lets us go eventually, offended that we have eaten so few bananas, offended also perhaps that we leave him empty housed and still empty handed.

The science teacher – I never did get his name – is dissatisfied with his lot. It seems to be a fairly common syndrome (I am thinking of Wanjella, an extreme case, and various others, the male teachers especially) of the educated youth of Kenya. They are left with an idea, perhaps, of how much there is to be had out there. They've been given a glimpse of another world and they can't – quite – get their hands on it. They are on the perimeters, neither one thing nor another. So they are fascinated by me – my whiteness, my choices – and yet they resent me. I am not comfortable with it. In fact I am ugly with it. There is something about it which makes me want to gloat:

See my Walkman. Look, touch, try it out. Dream. And hate me. By all means, hate me.

Because I think I hate you.

*

Abdi is a cousin of Nassir's. He's tall and thin, wears coordinating shirt and trousers, gigolo shoes, speaks English with a television-learnt American drawl. He works at the hospital and generally goes around with a smaller boy, another Somali with a good job and no outgoings, who dresses in just the same way. They wear aftershave. A pair of young dandies who look ridiculous in this cowboy town. But they're around. I see them a bit. They are experts at saying nothing.

Perhaps I will go to Nairobi in the school holidays, I say.

Ye–es. Nairobi. So you are going to go to Nairobi in the school holidays? That's nice. Nairobi is a very big city. Sometimes I go there and – ye–es. It's a very big city. There are lots of people in Nairobi, aren't there?

Abdi is leaning back, looking languid and beautiful (if it weren't for the shoes) and bored. Hassan is discussing a walk in the mountains he and Laura will be taking tomorrow while I'm at school. Abdi says, as he stares into the distance:

'I have a feeling it may be dangerous,' but he doesn't have the feeling, not really. He's just talking. Nobody pays any attention. He says: 'I find working is very difficult during Ramadan. Perhaps I will take a vacation.'

Then Bill joins us. He's smirking, standing on one of his tiny legs. He's looking at me. Obviously after something.

'Say, Daisy,' and his long cheeks look almost rosy, 'd'you have any perfume for a good cause?'

Good cause. Rubbish.

*

A muddle with the school timetable. I took a lesson which wasn't mine, so I arranged with the history teacher that she should take my English lesson in the afternoon. I was on my way out of the staff room, heading for another class, when she whistled to me. She was lying, cheek cooling on the boiling hot desk.

'You can take both lessons,' she said.

'But they already had two . . .'
'Yes. Take two.'

*

Laura's walk with Hassan was only partly successful. She pointed her camera at the mountains. There was a handful of Turkana women in the corner of the frame, about a hundred yards away and they turned on her. Charged. Started throwing stones. Hassan came to the rescue. Stood between the women and Laura and put a stop to it all. People don't like cameras in these parts. I should have warned her.

*

Jim Sweet has ordered me to cancel my evening lesson. He has arranged a little get-together for the Isiolo mzungus. Mrs Sweet is picking up some Ethiopian take-away from Kabede's wife, and bringing it to an American missionary's house a couple of miles away.

'Let's have spoons,' says Mr Sweet as the plates are passed around. 'It could get a bit messy.' Eating Ethiopian food with spoons is rather like pushing a bicycle downhill. Mr Sweet is missing the point. So he and his wife and an elderly Methodist preacher who, it turns out, lives in the next house to us but one, are given spoons. The American missionary and his wife, Tim and Connie, Laura, Bill and I, make a great point of eating with our hands, and the evening is a little grim.

Tim is native-converter.

'It must be a very good time for you, Ramadan,' says Laura, 'with everybody feeling so hungry.'

122

'Yes,' says Tim.

We discuss Laura's journey from London ('how adventuresome', says Mrs Sweet) and, at greater length, the cost of international postage.

The Methodist minister is a gentle, tired old man. He's been working in East Africa for the past forty years, but he has never adapted to the climate, or to anything about the place really. He is another one whose goodness is, if not inspiring, at least a little humbling.

We talk about Seileesh's palace (he gave me a guided tour this morning. 'And here,' he says, 'there will be flowers.' What? Dried flowers? 'No. Fresh flowers. Every day.') and the minister is suddenly quite violent. The money could be spent so much better elsewhere. He talks about the 1969–71 North Kenyan famine. It was Christmas Day and he'd found three bodies on the roadside. Picked them up, put dried soup into their mouths which they'd been unable to swallow. One died on the way to the hospital. One survived. One was sent to a refugee camp, still weak and was later eaten by hyenas.

'Super,' says Mrs Sweet from the sofa. She could have been talking about something else but the timing was unfortunate.

Nine-thirty and it is time to leave. 'I'm not wearing my dog collar tonight,' says the minister as we drive over the bumpy road to home, 'but that's because I was going to a party.'

*

Of course I have failed to fast . . .

My kitchen and Fauzia's living room are only about

five yards apart, so I crawl around, cutting up mangoes very very quietly, putting knives in the oven so she can see I'm not holding one when I'm standing up.

Fauzia prepares a feast every night during Ramadan. She sends a lot of it over the garden fence, via one of the children, to all of us. This evening came fruit and custard, chapati, curries, mandazi, avocado paste . . .

Achmed generally comes around soon after the food, saying he is bored of the television, bored of so much food.

'I saw the man with the Land Rover here yesterday,' he says tonight, 'I was going to tell you don't use him. He's expensive and he talks . . . But I thought I'll let him talk for a while first.'

*

I was explaining to Laura how she got from the house to town. We were walking home. I said, 'Oh, you'll recognise this bit. This bit's lovely. It's my favourite part of Isiolo.'

She'd been laughing and smiling up until then. I think I'd sensed that Isiolo wasn't really her idea of paradise. It never occurred to me, though, that she didn't love it a bit. But there was an outburst. Suddenly she lost her cool. She stopped me, in my favourite bit, turned to face me, said:

'You have to realise, Daisy, that Isiolo is not beautiful. I think your mind's warped. Daisy, Isiolo is a total pit.'

I thought she was mad at first, but then, now, all the ugliness keeps crawling back into my mind; the rubbish pits, the donkeys with sores, the goats with blood dripping down their legs, the men with boy's trousers on, too small to fit around their waists which leave their genitals to hang out of gaping flies. The smells, the roasted goats' heads, the street boys asleep in piles of rubble, so dirty that you pass by without even seeing them, the reek of the butcheries, the grimy cafes, the bland, starchy, monotonous food, the hideous, haphazard architecture, the half-built, then deserted houses. The shops which sell only Blue Band and curry powder, the dust, the incredible heat. The 'give me's', the endless calls of, 'Where are you going? What are you doing? Where is your cousin?', the children's chants, 'How are you? How are you? How are you?' to monotonous beat, high-pitched, careless voices, the calls of 'Mzungu, kuja!' – which expect to be answered, 'Kuja! Kuja! Kuja! – when I have other places to go. The 'give me your bicycle', 'give me lift', the men who put their weight on my handlebars and prevent me from moving away, only to say, 'So. Bicycle.' The need to cover your shoulders and your knees, always to be smiling, never to say 'stop – talking – fucking – rubbish', always to be good tempered, even when the people who pretend to be your friends overcharge you, the lack of privacy, the children tap-tap-tapping at the gate to be let in, the neighbours calling over the fence when you are trying to work . . .

But I do. I love it. I love Isiolo. I love to be here. I love the loneliness and the friendliness and the friendlessness and the terrible smells. I am happy here. I am very happy and very lucky to be here.

*

Laura pays for us to spend a weekend at the Hilton in Nairobi. We order enormous breakfasts, have baths, watch telly, drink wine, eat cheesecakes, lie by the pool, get clean sheets, read last week's *Times* in the guests' reception room, take afternoon tea. Do nothing. God, it is wonderful. My city fix. What a delight to see flashing lights, high-rise buildings. I lied to the school on Friday, told Mrs Tacho I had to leave early for Nairobi to renew my visa. She asked me to close the door (nasty moment), asked me if I thought the Sweets would be willing to sell her my bicycle.

★

I leave Laura in Nairobi and take the night bus back to Isiolo. A woman with a beautiful, fat baby and a well-worn breast sits beside me. When she sleeps she rests her head on my shoulder, but even in her sleep she is somehow timid. Every now and then she wakes with a start. Her head shoots up.

In the morning, my hair smells of poverty. I wash it.

★

'Owe-kaye,' says Bill, with the waxy grimace, 'there are one or two things I want to talk about. Something you said last week – you said "Bill's house – I mean our house" – made me think. Now I want you to understand that this is my house and that you are my guest. I want you to think of it like, you are my guest and you are *assisting* me a little . . . And another thing, these children in the house every evening. Can't you teach them somewhere else?'

Looks like it's time to move on.

★

So I go to see Kabede, tell him about Bill not wanting his children in the house and settle down for a satisfying bitch. 'It's ridiculous,' I say, 'I know our house is far larger than yours . . .' But the doctor decides to choose this moment to be gracious, and I've been waiting for it for so long.

'No, no,' he says, 'our children benefit. We must provide the room. I will talk to my wife. If my Mum goes we will have room. We can take the television out of the living room . . .'

*

Bill and I are avoiding each other. I look around the lodging houses in town to see what kind of a deal can be struck. It is a malicious move. News travels fast in Isiolo. I know Bill will find out. I know, when I move out, that it will not reflect well on him . . . Small diversions.

The Bomen quartered its price immediately but it's still too expensive. The Silver Bells man has an appalling stutter – the waiters annoy me there, anyway, and the room smells of mothballs. I can't be bothered to offer a deal there. It was hard enough persuading anyone to let me see a room.

*

I bump into a donkey in the throes of its agonising lament. Until now I had always imagined, when I heard the noise, that the poor thing was being attacked by lions. But no; he just stands there, with his bones, and wails for his existence. In mourning for his life. A philosophical animal.

I give a lesson at the doctor's house. He hasn't mentioned it to his wife, but still, the lesson goes ahead. Why does his mother always bow when she sees me? She carries a burning giko through the living room as my students discuss the various merits of London, Nairobi and South America.

The house smells of menstruation, but you get used to it. Or you get more than used to it. There is something about the matter of fact, solid, solid living that goes on in this tiny, tin-roofed house, the smell of the blood, the inescapable cosiness, the lack of pretence, the warmth . . . that reminds one: these mzungus, they're all as hard as nails.

Achmed calls me over to his living room. Fauzia is sick again, this time with a boil the size of a football on her shin. She can't walk.

'Is Bill giving you a – hard time?' he asks. He is clearly embarrassed. Bill has been complaining about me, about the broken plate. He has found out that I was making enquiries at the Bomen. And Achmed has found out that I'm paying Bill rent. (Actually, I told him.) He's very shocked. He's shocked that Bill is treating me so badly.

'Bill is very hard,' says Achmed.

'Ah well,' I say, 'perhaps he's not hard . . . These Americans, I don't know, sometimes they're a bit assertive about their rights. You know, I think they're taught to think a lot about themselves. It's not his fault . . . I think he's just got a little used to living on his own . . .' Tee hee hee.

Fauzia says she knows of a room ten yards up the road. 500ksh a month, no electricity, outside lav etc. She thinks it will be empty in a few weeks' time. She'll talk to the landlord. She can lend me a bed and a lamp and a giko. I can get a table and chair made by a man who lives behind the vegetable market for a couple of hundred shillings.

So that's excellent. It'll be good to have a place of my own, plus it's half the price of living at Bill's. And the stunted bastard can have his palace to himself again. I hope he is very lonely and I hope his legs grow even shorter. Meanwhile, very casually and subtley, I will set as much of the town against him as I can. It'll give me something nasty to do. Sometimes it can be a bit of a strain, always being so nice.

*

'Thank you for cleaning the bathroom,' he says, with a horrible smirk, on his way out to yet another safari. And I laugh but he doesn't get the joke. Term ends in a week. And I'll be off on safari myself. I think I will only assist him with the two weeks' rent this month.

*

I find Wanjella hanging about town. He's at a loose end. He takes me to a carpenter friend of his who will make me the table and chair. Says he'll get me a good price – 240ksh (£5).

'It must be very good timber,' says Nassir, later. Or perhaps Wanjella is taking a cut?

'This is strictly between you and me,' says Wanjella as we walk to the carpenter's house. 'But how much do sleeping bags cost?'

Bill bought a sleeping bag from one of his American friends, tried to sell it on to Wanjella at what seemed to me to be an exorbitant price. I can't remember how much he was asking, and I don't know how much sleeping bags normally go for but, take it from me, Bill was not being generous that day. He was asking Wanjella to hand over more than two months' salary. Bill refused to bring the price down, so Wanjella found himself a much cheaper sleeping bag in Nairobi. Bill had said that his was extra-specially superior, which I can believe, when I remember the idiots who carried it over . . .

So. Strictly between Wanjella and me, so far, regardless of the cost of a sleeping bag, I have found a bitching partner. At last. I'm very subtle, very casual of course. And I discover all sorts of delightful information. My two favourite pieces of which are:

1. That large (I say large) sections of the town are appalled, shocked, horrified, angered, outraged, by Bill's attitude to the local women. Poor, lonely fool, they only want him for the knick-knacks he supplies. Everybody knows that. Even Wanjella. I'm told that The Bill is going to get himself into trouble one of these days. (More about this later).

2. That there are people in his department, (though I'm never quite clear which department that is, or what work Bill is supposed to do. All I know is that he's often seen around town carrying cardboard boxes filled with scented Vaseline) who refuse to have anything to do with him. They say he is overbearing and tactless and rude and he always thinks he knows best.

'Yes,' I say, looking troubled, 'poor Bill. I think he is lonely. He seems to be very angry about something . . . Ah, well.'

*

Nassir is planning to set up a tile factory in Isiolo. At the moment only the army people, the very rich, have anything but corrugated iron, or cardboard, on their roofs. Tiles need to be brought in from Nairobi. But Nassir has found a way to produce the tiles at half the price. Something to do with materials being cheaper in the north.

'You will not be able to locate this house in five years,' says Nassir, with the miraa at the side of his mouth. 'Yes. Isiolo will be very large. OK, mwalimu. It is very late. I am going.'

And he leaves.

*

They call him the Professor because he is so clever, but he hates it. He escaped from Somalia, lost everything, arrived in Isiolo about the same time that I did. If he'd been on the other side of the country when trouble struck he could have gone north, to Saudi Arabia where he has relations with plenty of money. But he wasn't. He was on the Kenyan side and in Isiolo he has a cousin who owns a poor-man's hoteli, one that's so poor it can usually only afford to sell chai, mandazi and ugali. It runs at a loss and is always on the edge of closing. On the wall above the mandazi counter is a poster of an Arab woman in a one-piece bathing suit. There is a square cut out of the picture where her groin should have been and the filthy wall glowers through it.

Laura and I went there on the eve of Ramadan because all the other hotelis had run out of food. The Professor was very welcoming. Said he would be closing tomorrow, advised us to eat as much as we could.

But it is Ramadan now, and his is the only Moslem hoteli which still opens during the day. The Professor says they can't afford to close, says if they closed down for Ramadan they'd have to close down for ever.

I go there with Hassan, who is not fasting today because he chewed too much miraa yesterday. We eat mandazi that are almost as good as Fauzia's and the Professor sits down to join us.

He's a young man, or an old man, or a young man with a wise face and grey hair. He's a poet, and of course he knows his poetry by heart. So Hassan and I sit eating mandazi, and he leans on the table with one, curiously flexible elbow and his head is bent towards mine, but his body is pointed towards the till – you can't trust anyone around here – and his voice is lyrical, beautiful. He is chewing miraa and his eyes are bright with living. His body moves like the body of a young man. He is vital, alive, humble, humorous. He is the most extraordinary man I have ever met. He draws you into a spell, and he recites.

Hassan chuckles in the pauses because I don't think he's interested. He slurps on his tea, says, 'Ha ha, very funny. They kill him in Somalia. When he go back to Somalia they kill him. Like that.'

I learn, a little during this meeting, the rest during the many others, that the Professor was once an interpreter. He earned a good wage, lived well. Was sent to Moscow when the Russians were interested in Somalia. He's lived in Italy because the Italians were interested in Somalia too. But he's lost everything, including a daughter. His wife and surviving child are staying in Lodwar with her parents. He can't afford to keep them, so they must live apart. In Isiolo, in a simple, Moslem world, to be unable to support your wife is a terrible shame.

His poetry was published in illegal magazines in Somalia and as a result of them he was sentenced, *in absentia*, to death.

And so here he is in Isiolo, with nothing. Without, even, his wife. And the hoteli is near to closing and his books are burnt and his health is failing.

'But you can't eat words,' he says, and the laugh comes from his belly and he jumps up to discuss the price of tomatoes with a woman and a bucket-full who have just come in.

*

Good Friday. Fauzia says:
  'You are fasting today.'
  But I'm not.

*

An old man is leaning on a fence, somewhere between my house and the town, in the middle of nowhere. Three women are sitting on the ground. Their bui-buis are on the line, flapping in the wind.

'Jesus said,' he is shouting, shouting them down, 'Jesus said . . .'

But I don't hear what. He switches to Swahili and

I bicycle on.

*

Easter Sunday. I have bumped into the old Methodist minister on several occasions. Every time he asks me if I've been to Mass. I say no, grimace, think I can make a joke of it, and he smiles but he doesn't laugh. I don't know why I keep on expecting him to.

Easter Sunday and finally I am on my way to Mass. I bump into Kabede's family on the way back from their own service (I think they're Methodist; low church, anyway). I say:

'Good morning. Happy Easter. I'm just off to Mass.' I'm just off to Mass, but they're not impressed. They imagine, I think, that I'm just off to Mass all the time.

The Catholics are building a large church just opposite the track that leads to the Sweet's house, but it isn't finished yet and the service is held outside. It's very hot and there are ten people, plus babies, to every bench. I am next to a Turkana woman, in all the heat, and her hose-pipe bosom is feeding a baby, and the heat and the flies and the smell and the terrible crush and the length of the Mass and – there is something about my neighbour which makes her especially attractive to the flies – means that after an hour and a half I can stand it no more. I leave, and we haven't even got to Communion.

On the way back from Mass I pass a man in the street, squatting like a woman, pissing, through his rags and over his car-tyre sandals. I walk on.

*

Achmed has a three-inch razor cut across the top of his lip. He got it shaving. It's only the second time he has shaved in his life.

*

Henry is not asleep. He is leaning at his post talking to a young man I have never met before. We are introduced.

'Thissie ees a youngie neighbourie. You – er – you say "hellowie. How ees youie?" Er – that ees why you knowie people.'

So I say all that and then say goodbye.

'Ahh,' says Henry, 'you are nottie ready to be friends then.' So I stay and say hellowie again.

*

Isiolo's water supply has been cut off. Bill's house, apparently, has the largest water tank in the area, so there is a constant stream of people turning up with empty saucepans to fill. Henry shows a couple of friends to the outside tap. They are carrying four jerry cans between them.

'Yessy yessy,' he says. 'You justie – er – give them some water,' but they've taken it already anyway.

*

Laura, who came out here to decide whether or not she ought to get married, has sent me an invitation to the wedding.

*

There are no lessons during exams and I am suddenly bored by the small world I am living in, so I take my students' unmarked exam papers and set off for a day or two's safari around Kenya. I will return via Nairobi train station having picked up my mother, who is coming to call on me for a week. I can't really imagine her here, amongst all these strangers. I find it hard to believe that she will really turn up. It would be lovely if she did.

*

She does.

There seems to be a general feeling of approval and warmth towards mothers in these parts. She is given a grand welcome in Isiolo. Even Bill mends his manners for the first half hour.

Mr Job the Samburu jeweller comes to call, says he feels bad about having allowed Laura to leave town without offering her any presents. So he makes up for it by giving my mother two amber necklaces and about forty brass bangles. She is embarrassed, offers to pay for them, but he won't accept anything in return. She tells him of a shop selling African jewellery in Somerset, says she'll take the necklaces along there and see if she can persuade them to put in an order. (She does, much later, and they do. Whether or not Mr Job ever followed it up I have yet to discover. He hadn't by the time that I left.)

Mr Job tastes my mandazi, cooked in honour of Mum, and says they're not as good as Fauzia's, which of course they aren't, nor anywhere near. Fauzia's, as I keep saying, are the best mandazi in town. Mine are the second worst. He says Arab women are expected to cook well because that's all they have to do. That and look after the children.

Samburu women, on the other hand, do a good deal more.

'My Mum,' says Mr Job, 'cooks the food, looks after the animals, fetches the water, carries the firewood . . . And my father, he goes to the hairdresser. Sometimes he can spend four days. And then he looks be–au–ti–ful. Very very good, you see?'

Mr Job the electrician wears Western clothes when he's in Isiolo, but he's bought himself a plot of land near his village and he returns there often. When in Samburu land he does as the Samburus do. So I have never seen him in tribal wear, but I have noticed, recently, that his hair is growing extremely woolly. It sticks out all over the place these days and I wonder, now that we're on the subject of hairdressers, what's going on.

He's taken to washing it in Omo, a clothes washing powder which turns everything it touches into a sort of white cardboard. It cannot be doing Mr Job's head any good, but he says it's an essential hair-care process if he ever wants to get a style like his father's.

He stays and stays. I know he has been generous, but I wish he would go away. Now he is telling my mother that Kenyatta wasn't really a Kikuyu at all. He says that he happens to know that Kenyatta's official father, who was a Kikuyu, decided that in order to breed a man who might one day be king, or president, he had first to get the parentage correct. 'So he told his wife to make child with a Samburu because he knew they were more intelligent. And she had to obey.'

Please go away, Mr Job. Please. Go away.

He leaves within moments of Baby's arrival. Baby is Achmed and Fauzia's Turkana house girl. She cannot speak Swahili or English. We absolutely cannot communicate on any subject. At all.

Henry comes knocking at the door. 'Ye-es,' he says, 'I have – er – I have bring you a friendie. Here shee – er – is. Yes.' And he leaves me, holding the bloody Baby.

She sits down in the living room and giggles and doesn't speak. Oh, why is she here? When will she go away? I want to talk to my mother about clothes and cousins and architecture and – anything. Anything fancy at all. I don't care. I just want to use long words. Now.

Baby goes, eventually. These little irritations, they will always pass, but it's so hard to believe that when they're happening.

*

My mother is richer than Laura, and she's come all the way to Kenya. It would be a shame to go home without seeing the elephants. Time, then, to recall the odious chatterbox Mohammed. I ask Hassan if he can think of anyone else with a car (Seileesh isn't in town and besides, Isiolo is split, I think, between the Bill and the Daisy supporters. Seileesh wouldn't be that keen to help me out even if he were around), but Hassan says there is no one else. He'll get hold of Mohammed and we'll all meet at the Salama tomorrow morning.

In the meantime Mrs Sweet comes round to meet my adventuresome Mama. Things are not going well in her life. It has been decided that Mr Sweet's contract will not be renewed. Unless he can persuade his employers to change their mind, which is unlikely, he will have to pack up everything within the next two months and go back to the flat in Reading where he came from. No servants there.

*

I go to see Kabede about cancelling the evening lesson. I also want to ask his wife if she would mind cooking some Ethiopian food for my mother. (This is not a particularly unusual request. She runs a sort of occasional take-away.)

But his clinic has turned, overnight, into a shop. Kabede is a shoe vendor today.

It is assumed that, with the opening of another, more efficient and cheaper clinic up the road, Kabede just ran out of patients. Anyway, he now sells shoes. The clinic signs have been taken away and he is, as usual, in a very bad temper.

Nassir, the businessman, has worked out that Kabede can't now be making more than ten shillings profit a day (20p). People don't tend to buy many shoes around here – most people don't wear them – and there are an amazing, an absurd, number of shoe shops in the town already. Kabede is not popular, because he is Ethiopian, perhaps. More probably because he's bad tempered. When there is so much choice and the prices are always the same why should anyone shop with an irritable outsider?

'Kabede,' says Nassir. 'He must be in trouble.'

He has four children to educate, a family of seven to feed. He might perhaps be getting sent money from Ethiopian (immigrant/refugee) relations elsewhere. Who knows?

I meet the neat primary school teacher who also gives evening lessons to Kabede's children on his way into the shoe shop. He looks as neat and gentle as he usually does, but yesterday his ten-year-old daughter died of malaria. Kabede is organising a harambe to pay for her funeral.

*

I take the exam papers back to my classes and everybody, I think, except the girl with 88 per cent, who came top, comes up to the front to quibble with my marking.

I have made a mistake on one girl's paper. She should have two points more than I gave her. I pass her the class list, so she can alter the result I have down there and she ups herself by 48 per cent.

'I was confused,' she says. At least she gets the tense right.

And now I am surrounded. Forty children are pushing their papers towards me. Everyone has a complaint. And of course if I've made one mistake – well – then I could have made any number. I try to double-check each paper as it's pushed towards me but I can't. It's total anarchy. I ask everyone to sit down, to bring their complaints up to the desk one at a time. But of course they won't. I check ten more papers, find nothing amiss, tell everyone that if they make me re-check another paper and I discover that my marks are all right then I'll deduct ten per cent off their final result for being irritating.

Nobody pays any attention.

Finally, the girl with 88 per cent takes control.

'Madam!' she shouts, from the back, above everyone

140

else, 'these girls, they are cheating you.'

Oh God. 'Are they? Oh. Right. OK. That's the end of that then. No. Too bad. Everyone sit down. You'll just have to make do with the mark you've got. Sorry, everyone. Sorry.' And the bell goes for the end of the lesson and I run.

Back to the Salama to meet my mother, Hassan and the chatterbox Mohammed. It's still early, before nine o'clock. My other class has an exam this afternoon so I have the rest of the day free to look at elephants.

*

Mohammed, who lives with his mother, sends his passion juice back to the kitchen because it's too cold. He decides that he can't take his antibiotics with anything but lukewarm tea.

And we leave for Samburu. He talks neurotically, incessantly, all morning. About his health, a great deal about his health, about how rich he used to be when Isiolo was involved with the ivory trade (I had so much money and nowhere to spend it), about how he used to drink and smoke with Isiolo's senior army officers, about how he lost all his money after the ivory trade collapsed – although he wasn't involved in it personally. About how he gave up smoking and drinking, took a job at the primary school, about how he was born Christian, converted to Islam, then back to Christianity, then to Islam again, about his nerves, about being the only honest man in the town, about himself. Always about himself. And he speaks very fast, and he never looks you in the eye. Or he never looks my mother in the eye. He only talks to my mother. Hassan and I exchange glances. I exchange glances with my mother, but she is very polite, says:

'Oh really?' at all the right moments. Except that there never is a right moment. He seems to resent even the smallest interruption.

At the entrance to the National Park we pick up an old Somali woman. She sits with us in the back of the truck, won't even speak to Hassan, who is also Somali, of course, and even politer than my mother. And we drive along those hot, dusty roads. The bumps don't quite drown out Mohammed's monologue. We can hear it just well enough to know that all is well. He is still talking. And finally we see an elephant. It's on its own a couple of hundred yards away.

Mohammed stops, is preparing to drive closer when the Somali woman finally speaks. We must drive on, she says. The elephant – the Rogue Elephant – killed someone years ago which is why it's alone. It's been ostracised by the rest of the herd and it's bad tempered and very dangerous. You can recognise the Rogue, she says, not just because it's alone, but by the nick at the top of its right ear.

This is the first time Mohammed has stopped talking since we met. He is shaking, drives off in the opposite direction at maniac speed, and the Somali woman chuckles and falls back into silence.

*

It's growing late. I have been told, though I never did discover whether it was true, that anybody found in a Kenyan National Park after nightfall is liable to be executed. Shot on sight, Mohammed tells us. No excuses allowed. It's an attempt to put a stop to the poaching.

Police cars and helicopters patrol the thousands of miles of park every night, their drivers' machine guns set ready to fire.

Mohammed is telling us this with a mad, excited gleam in his lunatic eyes and he is driving up a very steep hill in the wrong direction at God knows what speed in search of the lions. The bottom of his clapped-out car is scraping along the bottom of the hillside as we look into the sunset, watch a few zebra canter away. Mohammed is cackling. And —

Clunk. The car judders. Stops. Its bottom has fallen off. We're in the lion department. The sun is going down and Mohammed is threatening an asthma attack.

Twenty minutes later it is dark. The car is a disaster. Mohammed is talking – at my mother – about Allah's wishes, about how white people can't always have it their own way. And he is shouting at Hassan who is under the car in the pitch-black, bashing at anything which he thinks feels appropriate.

A safari van passes. The driver asks if we're in need of any help but Mohammed screams at him, tells him to go away, tells him everything's fine which it clearly isn't. For some reason Mohammed is terrified. He's hysterical. Still, the driver moves on and we are left alone, with this maniac, in the real middle of nowhere. Nowhere, nowhere.

Hassan argues with Mohammed in Swahili about sending the driver away, and Mohammed turns his horrible attentions from my mother to him. They are under the car and we are sitting beside them, pretending to be useful. Mohammed says:

'What's that roaring? I can hear the lions.' He brings a bottle of water from the car, holds it up in front of my mother, says, 'This is all the water we have', and pours it, laughing, over his head.

So. It's quite frightening. Hassan finally mends the car. We pull burrs out of the madman's head and he loses his temper, again, because we're not doing it properly. Several hours later we drive home.

Mohammed is a coward. He cries when we reach the Park gate, sobs that he's back in a Free Kenya, that he is back where the Father of the Nation (President Moi – not an excellent father) will look after him again.

He drops the three of us off at the Bomen, waves goodbye with a hideous smile, says: 'Of course, I was only worried for you.'

And I never see him again.

*

Achmed drives an overload of potatoes north to Wajir and turns over his truck. He says he is very lucky to be alive, says he will never take potato-shaped objects on that road again. It's too dangerous.

*

Kabede's mother is leaving for Ethiopia. She wants to be reunited with the rest of her children, but the journey will be very dangerous. She could be killed and Kabede is begging her to stay with him until things are safer. She won't. She will leave, on the back of a lorry, to-night.

PART THREE

I wave a sad goodbye to my brave and energetic mother at Mombasa station, catch the train back up to Nairobi to meet Miles, my lover, who has finally agreed to come out from London to join me. He has brought with him an expensive camera and a handful of commissions from Associated Newspapers. We have spent my Easter holidays travelling around the country. (It marks, I think in retrospect he would agree, the beginning of the end of our relationship. We did not get on well.) And he has returned to Nairobi where he has found a house, a handful of generous hacks, various others. I have left him there, hanging out with the fast set (and the hacks) trying to get a visa for Ethiopia, which, in spite of everything, I hope he doesn't get, muttering about civil war in Ethiopia, I don't know what. He's a city boy. And he likes to be getting on with things. He spent one night in Isiolo, but that was quite enough. We will meet up for the odd weekend, I think. And I will probably spend some time with him before I go back to Britain.

And so I am back in Isiolo, alone again. It's about time. For the past few weeks things have been a bit too easy. I've been feeling a bit of a fraud.

But now I have plenty of friends and a very nice room in the centre of town which is all my own. And I feel as though I have come home. There is gossip to catch up on, friends to call on, work to do. I must find out from Zaidi whether my oven ever managed to cook anything . . .

*

'WEWE!' bawls Monica, mother of the fat mandazi-cooker Nancy, from beneath the fruit-selling tree. 'WEWE! KUJA!' She's livid with me because I've been on safari and she imagines, correctly, that I didn't bring her anything back.

'WHERE IS MY PRESENT? WHERE?'

But I have no present for her. So she shouts at me for not having brought any material from a woman, apparently a good friend of hers, who came calling at Bill's house a few months ago. Finally, I shout back, and laugh, and we clap hands, and laugh, and we part friends.

And the next time I pass her way I will be sure to give her something.

*

Nassir has taken over temporary management of the Salama. It is odd to see him there, behind the counter. He has told one of his younger brothers to resign from his teaching job in Wajir and is filling in until he comes. He should arrive within the next couple of weeks, which will leave Nassir, the businessman, free to concentrate on other projects.

The Salama (the Isiolo Hoteli has been long forgotten. I now go to the Salama at least three times a day, to mark

146

books, write my novel, learn Swahili. I treat it as my office. If people are looking for me, they will generally find me there) has been refurbished in my absence. There's a glass case on the front counter now which keeps the samosa warm, traps the flies. And beside it is a trophy, awarded to the Salama a few years ago, for being the best ordinary restaurant in the district twenty-five years after Independence.

But the mandazi are just the same. And the passion juice is still the best in town.

*

Zaidi says she never got around to testing the oven because it rained every day while I was away. And today the wind is too strong. And tomorrow her husband is coming from Nairobi . . . Maybe next week.

Ah well. It looks pretty, anyway.

*

I am sitting in the Salama marking some books. Hassan joins me looking bleary eyed, having just got up and having just told me so. I ask him if he's going to the school today to sign on.

'Yes yes,' he says, 'I have been.'

'But you just got up.'

'Yes. I have been at eight o'clock. They say come back tomorrow. Tomorrow never comes.'

*

I have stopped giving lessons to all the Ethiopian girls

except Grace, because none of the others really needs them. I want to concentrate on persuading Hassan (junior) to learn to read. Bill is away on safari, as usual, and I still have the key to his house, so I give the lesson in his sitting room. It is more convenient – and I know Henry will tell on me. I know it will annoy Bill that I have been here. I also know, because this is Kenya and everybody is more generous, less small minded about such stupid things, that he won't be able to complain about it to anybody. He will have to burn off his Western resentment all alone, in his great big palace, and nobody will be there to sympathise.

Hassan (junior) cries, he says, because I have moved away into the centre of town and I am very flattered. But perhaps it is easier to cry, at fourteen, than to admit you can't recognise the word RED, which, as he sobs, is set on a neat little card before him.

*

'Eh-huh,' say the gigolo boys, as they sit down to join me at the Salama. 'So you are here.'

Yup.

*

An 8.30 a.m. staff meeting has been called for the first day of term. Three teachers arrive by eleven. The meeting is put back to two, and by three enough people are here to begin.

We spend an hour discussing whether to rename the dormitories after:

Deciduous trees,

East African mountains,

North Kenyan provinces,
Kenyan animals.
I think we settle on the trees.
Last term's food bill still hasn't been paid. Suppliers
are refusing to send food this term unless they are given
a post-dated cheque. The new desks need to be paid for.
And so on.

There is a long discussion (brought to a ten-minute
halt while the science teacher opens our soda bottles
against the edge of his desk) about the new Dorm
Tidiness competition. (I have been made head of the
new dormitory, as yet unnamed and unused). It's allowed
to sleep eighty. 'Officially'. In fact it will sleep a hundred
and forty-five.

What should the prize be for the tidiness competition?

Someone suggests a bottle of soda and half a loaf
of bread for each girl, but it works out too expensive.
It is decided that at the end of every term the winning
dormitory should be awarded a goat.

The elderly Swahili teacher, who is thin and gentle
and serious and, I discover, keen on the sound of his
own voice, makes a twenty-minute appeal for teachers
to beware of tribal/religious prejudice among the pupils.
Some of the teachers listen, but he does go on. The soda-
bottle opener falls asleep.

*

The rainy season is over and Isiolo is dustier and windier
than ever. The effeminate seamster is back in his place,
greets me warmly, explains the bandana he wears lopsided
across his head.

'It is the dust, see, mwalimu,' he says, and roars with

149

laughter. I give him some dark glasses. The dust is so bad now that you can't go outside and keep your eyes open at the same time.

★

Kabede is being extraordinarily friendly. He says Grace has fallen in love with me, bursts into tears every night at the prospect of my going back to England. It's a little embarrassing, because poor old Grace is my least favourite of the extra-curricula pupils. She is so slow and so shy. I am very impatient with her.

She went to her father in tears, he tells me, while I was away with my lover. She shouted at him, asked him how, when he was such a rich man, he could stand by and allow me to move into a room with no electricity and no water.

Very embarrassing. Anyway, it turned out that the room Fauzia had mentioned to me wasn't available after all. My room in town is extremely pleasant. It has electricity, usually. Water, more often than not. And it is very clean.

Even more embarrassing, that very night I forget to turn up to her lesson. Kabede comes to my room in a terrible rage, leads me back to his shoe shop, to Grace, who is crying again. And then Hassan (junior) turns up, and he cries, too, because he still hasn't learnt his alphabet, because I'm not living at Bill's house any more. Well, it's grand to be loved, what-not. But this is ridiculous.

★

The seamster is making me a present.

'I want it to be very fine, mwalimu,' he says, 'so it will

150

not be ready for a week.' It was never ready. It was never quite fine enough. He disappeared towards the end of my stay and we never even said goodbye.

*

A fat monster of a man with a long shaggy beard is brought to my door. He is in search of Bill (who's away on safari again), asks me if I'll at least give him the keys to Bill's house. I do, in exchange for his passport. We meet later at the Bomen and are joined by Wanjella and the Indian builder with two thumbs. The builder buys us dinner.

'Chris', who is ex-vso, spends the evening telling me about the good dope you get in Cardiff, his bloody motorbike, ways to fiddle the DHSS, and I am ashamed of him. The man with two thumbs complains that he hasn't been paid by the council and, as a result, is unable to finish building the dormitory of which I am head. Chris doesn't address a word to Wanjella or to the two-thumbed builder all evening. Instead he tells me that what he misses most about his vso time is not being able to speak to the locals in Swahili.

The others leave. He says, 'Thanks for scoring me a free meal,' and goes to bed.

*

I call on the Professor for the first time after my long safari and he kisses me (tells off one of his waiters for greeting me too boisterously), puts papaya and banana in front of me – it's a treat to eat fruit or vegetables in a restaurant – says he'll be with me in a minute.

151

Returns soon afterwards with a very young Somali girl. She's eleven, very shy, very sweet, very pretty.

'This,' he says, 'is so you can see the other side of the coin.' She's from a traditional, nomadic family, has just been pulled out of school and circumcised. Her father is looking out for a husband and she could be married at any time.

It is a little awkward. Exhibit A: the other side of the coin. She doesn't want to be with me. She's terribly shy. But we talk for a while. I ask her if she will come and call on me, and she says she will but I know she won't. By now she is probably married, and childless because she is only a child herself.

*

Mr Job drops in and all I have to offer him is a slice of Dairy Lea, brought out for me by Laura. He takes it, swallows it like an aspirin, which is probably the best way and opens the conversation by complaining about . . .

Bill.

'He talks to me like he talks to Hassan. He says Do this, Do that. I want to say, "Bill – I'm a grown man". Oh, and he will go out with anyone, Daisy. And, you must know, a man who cannot stand still, always running, running, he is very lonely. He will make a bad father. Earhh – he will go with anyone – dirty girls. Even Borans.'

Rumour has it he was chasing a good girl recently, not dirty at all. Her brothers found out about it and took Bill aside, threatened him with a knife.

Mr Job has to go. He has a touch of malaria. And he has to travel back to Maralal to sort out problems with family land. 'Someone has just grabbed it. We are trying to sort it out peacefully.' He goes.

*

The Ethiopian children are all in very bad moods. I ask them how they enjoyed their holiday and they all say they hated it. Kabede had taken them up to Nairobi. Grace (officials refused her entrance into Kenya, which is why she arrived so much later than the others. She and her grandmother had to be smuggled across the Ethiopian/Kenyan border) needed to have her papers sorted. Moulu needs to see an optician. So he took all the girls with him and then ruined everything by bringing them back again twenty-four hours later. They arrived at supper time (stayed with an aunt), ate, went to bed, went to the optician and the papers office, came back to Isiolo.

'He thinks we will become bad girls if we go to Nairobi.' And that was the highlight of their holiday, so they are very angry with their father, but they daren't complain.

*

Lessons are cancelled this morning. The school is in disgrace. The Swahili teacher says the students ought to be ashamed of themselves, only he takes twenty-five minutes to say it.

He is talking at assembly, holding forth in his careful whisper, standing, tiny and erect, in the long grass. He talks and Mrs Tacho begins to fidget, to look around. The other teachers whisper amongst themselves.

The morning is spent tidying up all the dormitories.

Poor Hassan is being made to pay for his indiscriminate mzungu-loving. The other Dutch volunteer (I didn't know there was one, so he says, 'you know, the one with' – and tells me her number plate) has fallen in love with him. She told Abdi, the bangle boy who got married, that she would pay him to bring Hassan up to the house. Abdi told Hassan, who told Japan and now Japan is trying to make Hassan visit the volunteer with him, so he can collect the money. But Hassan runs every time he sees her approaching and Japan is getting on his nerves.

'She didn't used to come into town at all,' he says, 'and now she comes all the time. And she's going to be here in Isiolo for TWO YEARS.'

I bump into Peter whom I haven't seen for ages and he is unusually friendly. He says he is going to Lamu soon, asks about buses to Mombasa, reminds me that he owes me 200ksh and I say oh no, no, don't worry about it and he says oh yes yes, I will give it to you very soon. More conversation about Lamu and then . . .

'Now, Daisy, I am very broke at the moment. Can you lend me 20ksh.' I laugh and so does he. Of course I can't. Horrible boy.

Hassan tells me that Peter's Japanese girlfriend sent him a letter the week before last. She enclosed some money to cover the cost of his bus fare to Nairobi. They were supposed to meet there last Monday. She was going to take him on safari to Tanzania, to Mombasa, to Lamu. But he spent the money on beer, missed the deadline and is now trying to raise some more so he can meet up with her in Lamu, though he has no idea when – or even if – she will still be going there.

★

The Danish volunteer has finally managed to lure Hassan into her house. She burst into tears as soon as he arrived, he tells me, and declared great love. Hassan, it seems, was rather angry.

'I say, "I go to Moyale. You not see me for two years." She is too old.'

Japan doesn't seem to think so. He has taken to visiting the poor woman every day. He tells her there are no tourists, that nobody wants to buy his bangles and he asks her for money, which she gives him, every day.

★

Achmed is back from Mombasa. Bill is dropping in between safaris. He is changing the fuse in Achmed's television.

'What would you have done if I hadn't been here?' says Bill with another long-cheeked smirk.

'But I was mending it when you arrived.'

Fauzia asks him if he is going to marry Fatima, the girl of the moment (actually of several moments. He's been seeing her for about a month), and Bill says he can't because she doesn't speak English.

'I might come and watch the news with you tonight,' he says, as if he were offering some tremendous honour, but Achmed and Fauzia are (relatively) cold.

155

Mr Job has a malicious gleam in his eye, having just left Bill in a filthy temper and quibbling with a couple of Boran girls over a bottle of perfume.

'I say, "Bill, you give these African girls too much money, too much perfume." He say, "Oh, it keeps them busy".'

He has finally offered to pay Mr Job for the amber necklace he's been keeping for three months. He says he will give him an old torch and 400ksh. The torch can be bought new at the market for 35ksh. Mr Job's necklaces usually go for between 750–800ksh. So Mr Job is angry. He has told Bill that he can keep the necklace for nothing and he has vowed never to make any deals with him again.

★

Mr Sweet is generally well-liked in Isiolo. He keeps himself to himself, is very English, very white. But he always pays his debts, tips correctly, buys jewellery, etc etc. He took a couple of amber necklaces from Mr Job a few months back, said he would pay him for them the following week. So a week later Mr Job visited Mr Sweet's office and asked for the money.

But Ali, the bad bangle boy and the best friend of Japan, had found out about the debt earlier, been to visit Mr Sweet, collected Mr Job's money and disappeared from town for a week or two on the proceeds. Mr Sweet had to pay for the necklaces twice over.

★

Mr Job and Hassan sit in my room arguing about the beauty of the women in their various tribes. Somali women are famously beautiful. Mr Job is onto a loser. He says, from beneath the Omo-soaked rug, 'But not only Somali women have soft hair. Fuck off.' Samburu women are tough, solid, built for hard work. Their husbands aren't bad looking, though. Not at all. (I don't say so. No. Bad taste.)

They discuss the advantages of polygamy:

'It is good to have two wives,' says Hassan, 'because they compete for each other. But four or five is bad because then they are together and they are always complaining.'

*

Achmed comes to call, says Fauzia is shy, won't come to visit me (I live off a courtyard. It's a lodging house) because of the prostitutes who rent out the neighbouring rooms. 'Sometimes she is too religious,' he says and he laughs.

He is taking Henry to court for stealing 600ksh worth of food. Achmed sent him off, with a 50ksh tip for delivery, to fetch the ingredients that his wife would need while he was away in Mombasa. But the food never materialised. Henry kept the money and the food and, stupidly, stayed at his watchman's post. Achmed says he wouldn't bother taking him to court but for the fact that he had done it so many times before. And now he's looking for a new guard. He's bought a plot of land behind Bill's house and the materials (he plans to build the house himself) will be arriving next week. But Henry won't guard them, he'll steal them. Achmed says Henry is a drunk. I have never noticed it, but then Henry does seem to spend most of his time asleep.

*

Have tea with the Professor and the two-thumbed builder in a dirty, Christian hoteli. The builder is hot, and depressed about the state of the nation. He complains about Moi in a whisper and the Professor disappears to go to the toilet. Half an hour later he has not returned. I go to buy some cigarettes and find him, rubbing his hands together, striding up and down the corridor outside the lavatory. He is distracted, doesn't see me and his face looks old and miserable.

*

The Professor is sick and I cannot see him.

Hassan is angry with Bill because of a bad deal over a necklace which Bill now refuses to honour. Hassan is not like Mr Job. He says, 'But now I know how to pay him.'

He has plans to get even, all of which involve over-charging him for various services.

*

I bump into Esther who tells me there are some people waiting to see me back at my room. I forget about it, come home two hours later and they are still there. Five little children with school books and a gabby old man with no teeth and a stick. I have never seen them before.

'Lessons,' say the children.

The old man points at me. He is smiling, says

'Mwalimu'. Nobody can speak English so I explain to them in my fourth-rate Swahili that I am very busy now, but that if they return at the same time tomorrow I'll give them a lesson then. They leave, still smiling. But perhaps they misunderstood. I always think my Swahili is clearer than it is. They don't turn up the following day and I never see the children again.

I see the old man, several times, and each time I ask him what happened to the children, but he only smiles, and I never understand his reply.

*

Hassan spends the evening with an Englishman who speaks Swahili as well as he does. He comes to see me from the Bomen, where the two of them have been chewing and drinking beer for several hours. He is suddenly irritated by my inability to learn the language, starts gabbling at me very fast, says he is only going to speak to me in Swahili and Somali from now on.

So, we are sitting outside my room, looking out onto the life in the courtyard. Hassan breaks off his impatient, incomprehensible language lesson, whispers: 'See. That is two man for one lady.'

And we watch them, time them making a deal, make bets on which one will get first turn, see the other one go off for a beer and return, hang around in the courtyard until the first man comes out of the woman's room —

And Hassan forgets about the Swahili lesson, talks instead about how one day he will be rich, and it is a blessed relief.

A 'delegation of headmasters' is to visit the school next week. I have been told that I must attend.

*

Golden Finger – nobody knows his real name, they call him Golden Finger because he's such a crook – is lying in the shadows outside the Salama.

'I am lying here,' he says, 'because Isiolo is too hot.' He sits up and I join him down there. He tells me that he has had malaria, which is why he has cut his hair, that he has a headache because he's been doing too much disco dancing, that Somalis (he is Somali) are in fact Asians, not Africans, which is why they love white people so much, that he has spent all his money on beer and that he is very hungry.

We go to eat. He points to an old madman who is shuffling across the road. 'That man,' he says, 'come from very good family. He went to university. He want to go America. Then he is mad and now he live on streets. Very sad. Very very sad.' And then he stands up and begins to move his tiny, fine-boned body, his snakey hips, to the Somali music playing on the loudspeakers overhead. He is an incredible dancer.

*

The American Peace Corps has come to town. Bill is giving a weekend party to which, needless to say, I have not been invited. Kabede's wife is cooking for them tonight. Hassan has disappeared to sell them bangles.

*

I bump into one of the Peace Corps boys in town. He says he plans to stay on in Isiolo for a few days because Bill has told him about the beauty of the Somali girls. The two of them hope to spend tomorrow night carousing down in Boulapaissa – the poorest part of Isiolo and where most people live. Most of the houses are made from cardboard, milk cartons, sacks, stuff like that. An old age pensioners' section, built from mud and grass by younger members, which is set slightly apart from the other buildings. (Bill and his friend won't be stopping off there.) It looks like an African village in a story book. Very pretty.

*

The watchman at my hotel is a rugged, bad tempered old man. He sits in a corner with a fisherman's mackintosh on, though it is always unlikely to rain. He carries bundles of miraa wherever he goes and when he tears at them with his teeth it reminds one of an elephant eating a tree.

Anyway, he has been given a day or two off work to mull over his position. Last night he was caught red-handed stealing miraa from a lodger's bedroom. Bernard, the young man who manages the lodging house, has brought in an enormous – at least seven foot by seven foot – replacement, who sits in the old man's chair and says nothing. He wears a very smart red and black uniform.

*

A drunken old man puts his head through my window

as I sit at my desk. He belches and makes my papers flap, says:

'Seesta! Now I am go for a walk.'

Bernard leaves his algebra (he works on his algebra every evening) to shoo the man away and I am grateful, although I could have done it myself.

Bernard often has to shoo strange men away from my door. I'm a bit of a sitting target. Then he comes into my room says – always the same thing – 'You call me if there is trouble'. He is very protective – too protective really, but then perhaps I have grown complacent. Perhaps I am more vulnerable than I think.

*

There was an enormous fight in the courtyard at three o'clock last night. A passing drunkard provoked a fight with the crooked watchman (who has now returned) and the watchman took off his mackintosh to punch him. A prostitute, also drunk, slumped against the wall and whimpered. The police were called in. Ten of them arrived, all with rifles, and the woman began to scream. She walked up and down the courtyard, up and down, wailing and screaming. The drunken man smacked her in the face, but otherwise nobody paid much attention to her. A crowd gathered outside to watch what was going on. The man was arrested and I went back to sleep.

*

The 'delegation of headmasters' arrive five hours late. There are only two of them. I disappear. If they see me they might ask questions and my position here is very unofficial. I don't want to be sent home.

*

The British High Commissioner stops off at the Bomen on his way back from the North. He is wearing a monocle.

'He is very rich man,' says one of the waiters afterwards. 'If he wears one grasses he is very rich man. He must be a Rord or a Sir.' Or a wanker.

*

Nassir introduces me to a friend and I shake hands with him, although he seems reluctant. I am told that he (the stranger) has just eloped with his fifteen-year-old bride. Her parents disapprove, because Nassir's friend, the bridegroom, comes from a different clan. She is now being kept in hiding in Kisumu by one of his aunts.

'I don't know if you know,' says Nassir, very tactfully, very gently, after he has gone, 'but you're not supposed to shake hands with a man, especially on Fridays if he's going in that direction.' (It is a Friday and the man was going in that direction, towards the mosque). 'He will have washed his hands to pray, you see? And now he will have to do it again.'

And I've been here all this time and I didn't realise. And everyone is so polite that they haven't told me. And soap is so expensive in these parts, but Nassir only laughs, so perhaps it is not as embarrassing as I think.

Nassir and I were discussing computers – he has just bought a brand new Apple Mac, which he hasn't tested – couldn't possibly test. All he knows is that it's called an Apple Mac and that it comes with a television screen

– from a Somali refugee who'd smuggled it through the Kenyan border and was desperately in need of some money.

Hassan was there, laughing, interrupting every now and then to remind us of the size of Japan's belly ('He wears his T-shirt OUTSIDE! ha ha ha'). Then he stood up. 'Your computer story is too long,' he says, 'now I'm going to the cinema.'

That was lunchtime. Nassir and I had arranged to meet again at four o'clock. He was carrying a branding iron and was on his way to stamp his initials on the ten cows he bought yesterday. He asked me if I would like to come and inspect them.

But it is now seven and he still hasn't turned up.

*

I teach Fauzia how to cook banana and honey shortcake. She has a set of Bill's house keys (so do I, in spite of his repeated attempts to get them back. I only keep them because I know it irritates him) and we use his oven. Henry catches us in there and will tell tales no doubt.

Fauzia says of Bill, 'I begin to think bad thoughts of him', and I say, 'Aahh, yess, we–ell'.

That evening Bill slides an odious message under my bedroom door:

Daisy,

Please bring the keys tomorrow afternoon. If I am not there leave them with Fauzia. Bill.

I ignore it.

I gather that two old Somali men have been overheard threatening to report Bill to the police for chasing their women. I don't know if it's a crime, but then, I suppose, anything could be in Isiolo.

*

The Ethiopian president has done a runner. The rebels have taken over Addis Ababa, ammunition dumps are exploding in the centre of the town and Miles is reporting it all for the *Evening Standard*.

I go to discuss the situation with Kabede, who is angry at the inference that the situations in Somalia and Ethiopia should be compared. He says:

'There is no looting and no raping in my country.' But he is kind, asks me to ask Miles, if I get to talk to him, to send a message to one of his relations. But I don't get to talk to him. Of course not. It's an unrealistic request.

He says that Grace cried when she heard the president had run away. The same president who had kept her apart from her family for three years. 'But you see she has only ever heard that he is good,' says Kabede and then he leans closer, whispers, 'it's like President Moi and the children here.'

*

Hassan has been chewing. He is telling me about Wanjella who, apparently, used to pretend to outsiders that he was in the army and then take money off them. He is talking with a great deal of energy. And he can't draw breath when he's been chewing. He just can't stop.

The old watchman shuffles past, leans his head through the door, says: 'Speak slow-ly,' and shuffles away.

He's quite cool, the crooked watchman.

*

I wake up in the middle of the night because a bright torch is shining in my eyes. I look up just as the curtain falls back and I am quite frightened.

In the morning I discover that my Walkman, stupidly left by me on the desk beneath the open window, has disappeared. I am suspicious of the crooked watchman, so I ask Bernard to make gentle enquiries, which he does.

The watchman says he'd pulled back the curtain in the middle of the night because he thought he heard a noise. Yes, he'd seen the Walkman there but no, he certainly hadn't taken it.

So the following evening the watchman and I are not as friendly as usual. We ignore each other. And in the morning I find the Walkman back where it belongs. The watchman keeps his job. I pretend to think that it must have been there all along, buy him some beer and some miraa and I think that we are friends again.

*

Wanjella comes to call, along with various others. My room has become something of a general hanging-out pad for anyone who is bored in the neighbourhood. This evening my guests are discussing lorries and on the whole I sit in silence. Wanjella asks me to help him write out his CV and asks me to dinner the following evening.

Everybody laughs once he's gone. They tell me to be careful, that Wanjella is barking mad, that his CV is made up of lies and that he doesn't stand a hope in hell of getting the job he is applying for.

166

Another salon session in my waterless cube. The Professor is here, a couple of the male teachers, Nassir, Mr Job. We are discussing democracy, or Kenyan democracy. They are agreeing with each other about what a marvellously well-run democracy Kenya's is and the music on my tape comes to an end. There is a moment's silence. I have been listening to them, hearing them agree that President Moi is a wonderful man because he gives a beggar a lift to the hospital, buys him mandazi, issues a bloody press release to tell his people all about it. The door and window are opened onto the courtyard and for a second I forget where I am. I forget the rules. I suppose, when you come fresh to the sort of injustices to be seen daily in a place like Kenya, you are more easily shocked, less philosophical about it perhaps. I say – I shout –

'But you're all mad. Kenya is NOT a democracy'.

And it can be heard out there in the courtyard, in all the open-windowed rooms off it, where the army boys and their prostitutes lie. My companions – all of them – freeze. Turn white. Then the Professor leaps towards the tape recorder and switches the music back on.

'Daisy,' he says, '*Daisy!*'

The teachers reach for their cigarettes, disagree with me in feeble voices. They are leaving. But Nassir is already at the door.

'No,' he says. 'I am not here. I am going now. I am going now. I cannot hear this.'

And the Professor turns to him, with fear, with a gleam of manic humour in his eyes. He says:

But you're one of – them.'

'No. I am going now.' And he leaves. The teachers

leave. So does Mr Job. The Professor stands up to go. He laughs. He is almost himself again.

'Daisy,' he says, 'you went too far. You can't talk like that.'

And I am left alone.

*

Wanjella arrives punctually the following evening, absurdly punctually. He is dressed in black tie and a white, frilly shirt.

Oh dear. He does look stupid, in the middle of this cowboy land, with his ugly face popping up above the frilly shirt and I don't think, in retrospect, that I was very kind to him.

But then it's not me who is breaking his heart, it's my money. And he is not a very nice or honest or attractive man.

Dinner doesn't last long. I am not comfortable, don't feel entirely secure. He cross-questions me about the West and I feel sure that, any minute, he might ask me to marry him.

So. Instead he asks me to ask Mr Sweet if he will sell – me – his computer. For some reason he doesn't want to ask Mr Sweet if he can buy it himself. But he can't type. He has no money. He has no need for a computer.

'What else does Mr Sweet have?' he asks. 'I would like to buy it.'

I say of course I will ask Mr Sweet – anything he wants me to ask him. But I have very little intention of doing so. And I go home. I think I have offended him, but then, actually, I think he has offended me too. He won't be asking me to dinner again.

The Professor is angry and very sick. He is sitting in a corner of the hoteli unable to breathe. He says he can't go to bed because every time he goes to bed one of the waiters – they are hired by the day – steals all the money in the till. Yesterday they took 1800ksh. Today the hoteli can sell me nothing but chai – they have no money to buy other ingredients.

He leans across the table, puts his hand over mine, gasps out – he is clearly in pain – that he needs money to keep the hoteli alive. The humility with which he asks is quite horrible, finally, quite humbling – but not yet. The young white girl, still – always – from Ladbroke Grove, who knows nothing of hunger except that which is self-inflicted, who knows nothing of anything but good times, really, to whom – say, three thousand shillings – is nothing, maybe a slightly smaller wood carving for one of her family members back home sits there with her fresh, optimistic face, listening, through the wheezes, to this old, brave man, old, brave poet. And she waits for him to finish, although she knows what he is going to ask. She waits until he has gasped it all out. And she is so – ludicrously – happy to be asked.

Nassir has sent his younger brother to Nairobi with the Apple Mac. He was supposed to be taking it to an expert to get it valued, to see whether or not it still worked. But the younger brother (Mohammed) left Isiolo a couple of days ago and Nassir has heard nothing. He is going up to

Nairobi himself now to find out what's going on.

*

The gabby old man who brought his children/grand-children for lessons turns out to be some sort of relation to the owner of my lodge. This afternoon he is sitting in the crooked watchman's chair. He summons me over to tell me that the watchman has been severely reprimanded for putting his torch through my bedroom window.

*

There's been a donkey wandering about for the past few weeks which looks even sicker than the rest. It's been getting steadily worse. Mr Job says he advised – whoever it is should be advised – that it be put down. 'It's a health hazard,' he says.

Anyway today it must be even more of a hazard. It is lying on its side, with flies at its wounds, giving off the most appalling smell. It's dead, I think.

*

Dinner at the Sweets. There are a couple of whites there who've come down from Nairobi. After supper we are given a slide show.

Pictures of the kids playing badminton on the lawn.

'Did you get some people up to be ballboys?' says one of the guests.

A picture of a couple of women in G-strings playing softball on a beach in South Africa.

'Yes,' says Mr Sweet, and nobody laughs, 'that's a very

interesting game people tend to play on beaches.'

'Super,' say his wife and the other white woman, in tandem.

*

Kabede has given me a million messages to give to Miles to give to his sister. I have to ask how the bit of Addis in front of the Pepsi Cola factory, beside the cement factory looks. He says he wants to go back to Ethiopia to fight for his clan, now. He is looking for sponsorship for his children. Would I be able to get any for them back in England?

*

A blind man is led into the staff room by the talkative Swahili teacher this afternoon. The teacher holds him ever so gently and asks in his irritating, softly-softly voice, if people would like to make a small donation. Which they all do, every one of them hands over a fraction of their hardship allowance. Every one of them does it with the same ghastly, sensitive smile. The staff room suddenly reminds me of home. I am surrounded by these odious expressions, these people pretending to care. There's a fucking 'differently abled' person every three centimetres in this town. And here was one, fat blind man with a self-pitying face and he is being smothered with patronising gentility.

I don't make a donation. I walk away.

*

Japan has malaria. Nassir has returned from Nairobi with a cold ('I think a cold is worse than malaria', he says) and a worthless Apple Mac. His brother opened the box which said:

DO NOT UNDER ANY CIRCUMSTANCES OPEN THIS BOX.

So it broke.

*

Dinner at Mr Job's. He says he has reservations about cooking for a woman, but he gives me delicious ugali and stew. He shows me his jewellery – keeps trying to give it to me. Opens a cardboard box full of sun oil and makes me take that instead. He hands me a stick – it's a root of some kind, I think – takes a plateful of ash from the giko and shows me how to clean my teeth. Works far better than smokers' toothpaste. I leave his house with a brighter smile than I've had in years. The same root, when it's made into a stew, he tells me, can improve a woman's fertility.

Mr Job walks me most of the way home but he stops when we reach the busiest part of the town.

'I don't want to be seen with you at this late hour,' he says and leaves me alone.

*

Hassan still hasn't signed up for the school, but he has worked out a plan to get the money from the American boys just the same. He says he will use the money to buy cattle. Then, when he is rich, he will go to school very quickly for one year – in case his benefactors want to see some certificate of education . . .

I don't think it will work but he is filled with optimism.

*

I have finally got it together to visit the cinema. A cranky old television plays music videos in a crowded little room. They are interrupted by advertisements for theme parks off the M25, home delivered milk. Then the screen goes dead. We watch ten minutes of a film with Greta Scatchi and Tom Conti and the screen goes dead again. Back to the music videos. Back to my room.

*

Hassan is having a fling with an English tourist called Lucy. She is travelling in a group of three – I haven't seen them. The other two girls are apparently making a great nuisance of themselves. Last night one of them knocked on Hassan's bedroom door because, they said, they needed to ask Lucy where she'd put the lavatory paper. She was the one who'd used it last.

*

It is Independence Day today. I am advised not to venture onto the main street or I'll be rounded up by the police and forced to go to the sports field to listen to the DC's speech.

*

Mr Job comes to call. He was meant to go back to Samburu today, but they wouldn't let him put his timber on the bus. So he has brought his timber with him to my room and is waiting here for a different bus to come in. This bus, which should be leaving in the morning, will be left empty overnight. Mr Job will load his timber when nobody is looking and go up to Samburu tomorrow.

Before he leaves he takes me to visit a Samburu family in Boulapaissa. The young girl, he says, will teach me to make beaded bracelets. I'm not that desperate to learn and it is very inconvenient for him, but there you have it. It's a tangled web, etcetera, we start weaving when we get into all these good manners.

The Samburu girl – she can't be more than fifteen – speaks no Swahili or English. She lives in a cramped and dirty tin hut with two old men, one of whom, presumably, is her husband. The men sleep. I stare at them, at nothing, into the grimy half-light and long for an excuse to leave. But then, even if I had one, she wouldn't understand what I was saying.

She threads beads onto a piece of string which is too thick for the holes and her rough hands are too clumsy for the job anyway. She doesn't attempt to teach me. Perhaps she is too shy. Perhaps she thinks, as I do, that beyond getting the right thickness of thread, there isn't really very much to learn. I sit there for two hours. Then she mimes to me that the string is too thick for the holes. I try to look disappointed and surprised.

Escape.

*

Nassir's niece, who runs a hairdressing salon in Meru (Bill goes there – I think she's an ex) has married a man without asking permission of her father. Her father is telling everyone that he's going to kill her.

*

Another robbery at the lodge. This time the thief had to have had a key . . . But the watchman stays. He's been calling me his daughter ever since I gave him the beer etc and I don't mind at all. We are very friendly with each other again now. He thinks that all my visitors are lovers (and I must have at least twenty visitors a day) so he keeps laughing and winking at me; Us Rogues Together. He Won't Say Anything. He must be the worst guard in the world.

*

There is a feud going on between the Somalis and the Boran. A couple of Somalis were killed just outside Isiolo last night. Japan, a Boran, swears he will kill all Somalis but Hassan continues to be a good friend.

*

The Somali refugee family being supported by Nassir were arrested last night for not being able to speak Swahili. They will be freed when somebody comes up with enough money.

*

A couple of vso people are staying in Isiolo tonight. One of them, called Phil, is sleeping in the cube next door to mine. He sits on my bed and tells me about himself.

He talks about his feminism, his attitude to the Africans, his trail of self-discovery, his level of fulfilment and I am delighted for him. At midnight Hassan, for some perverse and, I suspect, slightly malicious reason of his own, arrives with a very drunken middle-aged woman from Bradford. She stands in the middle of the room and shouts about her sex-life – or lack of it. And Hassan stands behind her pulling faces and giggling.

*

Zaidi hasn't managed to try out the oven yet. A friend of hers had a baby.

*

The tourist season is in full swing. Mzungus everywhere. Last night a gang of eight Japanese took over a couple of rooms in the lodge. They switched their lights off and chanted for several hours before supper. According to the crooked watchman they are a Christian group doing a tour of church services in Africa.

*

Hassan is drunk and I am high on miraa, so perhaps we are not making much sense. Poor Hassan has been awaiting the return of Lucy for a week now. She was supposed to be stopping off in Isiolo on her way back from the North, but it looks as though she has given it a miss. Hassan cannot stop talking.

'I know when I drunk I can't start talking and sometimes I think I stop before this man tell me – but then I can't . . .

Men with hairs can be very strong and very rich. Me, I have hairs and when they are wet veerryy good. Then when they are dry they not straight Ha Ha Ha.'

★

Golden Fingers has taken to following me around rather. He tells me:

1   which languages he speaks,
2   that he left school in stage four because he loved discos,
3   that Somalis, like Arabs and Indians, are in fact mzungus,
4   that he's hungry . . .

★

Kaminasi is a pest. He keeps selling me bad bangles for bad prices and I can't get rid of him. I've saved you from him until now. He's an older bangle-seller with a reputation for brigandry. He goes around town telling everyone that he comes from a very rich family who will one day give him all their money and then he beats people up if they don't appear to believe him. Anyway, he's found out where I live now. He knocked on my door this afternoon while I was sleeping. Wouldn't go away until I bought this stupid brass rhino which fell apart in my hands as soon as he walked away.

Bernard (the lodge manager) says he will laugh if I am robbed again. It will serve me right for talking to people like Kaminasi.

★

The Somali refugee family, having been freed when Nassir paid the appropriate bribe, has been arrested again. Nassir who, along with the two gigolo nephews, is sitting in my room discussing lorries when the news arrives, leaves for the police station to free them again.

'Mmm. It'ss-teerrible. I- w-ishshsh I could he-elp,' says the taller and more irritating of the gigolos.

But Nassir seems to help everyone. He is an extraordinary, unsentimental man. I asked him once, because every time I see him he is talking of a new, money-making scheme, what he would change about his life when the real money started pouring in. He was a little shocked, I think.

'No, mwalimu,' he said (from behind the ever present twig of miraa, from beneath the eyelashes, the constantly surprised forehead, the miraa-encouraged, eternally alert and honest brown eyes), 'I do not need all these things. That would not be right – to have all these things when other people need more. You see?'

And he says it so simply and lives by it so unfussily, I am silenced.

★

A crowd of very cheerful-looking students are walking down the school drive as I walk up it. They have been sent home and will not be allowed back until they have come up with their school fees.

★

Nassir has an idea which he hopes will attract more tourists to Isiolo. He wants to build a mock Somali village just beyond the hospital so people can see how the Somalis really live. 'You have a camel – seeing a camel milked is very important to mzungus, you see?'

The idea has been made to work for other tribes in other parts of Kenya. So there is no reason why it shouldn't work here.

*

We have a debate in one of my classes about contraception. Altogether, thirty-eight of my forty-five students believe that any form of contraception is wrong. Using contraception, they say, makes a woman more liable to turn to prostitution. It helps to spread sexually transmitted diseases (I put them right on that one). Anyway, God said we should fill the world with people. And the fewer children we have the more likely it is that they will all die and we will finish up with none.

The class discussion which compares Western to traditional life styles becomes so heated that the teacher from the next-door class has to ask us to quieten down. Half the class is in favour of clitorectomy; they say it teaches a girl obedience.

It is very hard to mediate. I try to remain impartial but when I leave the room my mind is reeling.

*

The crooked watchman's mother is sick today and Bernard, the young manager, has taken his place. He is dressed in a very neat, very white, belted anorak and he sits with his knees together on the watchman's chair nibbling at a twig of miraa. It's hard to believe he could even frighten the rats away.

He calls me over, asks if he can borrow 100ksh to buy some spot cream –

★

Issac, who works at the bank, is a good friend of Nassir's. He's gentle, intelligent, humorous, hard-working, obsessed with foreign politics, the future of Africa and who is to blame for its present. He's good company. I am always pleased when he comes to call.

Today he is sitting neatly on the chair I bought in Kisumu, talking gently, though perhaps with a mild intention to bait, about Africa's right to be compensated for the slave trade. I disagree, not so gently; the dust and the fact that my lodge has been waterless for a week are making me irritable. I say women have been exploited far more and for much longer than the African has and that if there's any mass compensation to be had – which I don't think there should be, because it's silly – then, clearly, women must be at the front of the queue.

Issac is silent for a minute. He says:

'But how have women been exploited? Women are not exploited.'

I laugh, a little hysterically. My students' lines on obedience and prostitution have been banging around my head. My anger at the women's passiveness here has been so strictly controlled for so long, but I am leaving Isiolo soon and the West and my freedom in the West have been looming larger, more realistically. I am beginning to have a feeling, now, that a great weight will be lifted from my shoulders the day I take the last bus to Nairobi, to home, to people who don't question the exploitation of women.

'Well,' I say, ha ha ha. 'God. I can't even believe

you're asking me this.'

'No. Women are not exploited. A good man looks after his woman –'

'OK. OK. Ha ha. We can start with CLITO-RECTOMIES!'

He pauses. 'Yes,' he says, 'I am against that. It is not so enjoyable for the man.'

Oh, dear God. Take me home.

*

Nassir tells me that Bill never got around to organising who should pay for the lunch, held at the Salama ages ago for the American Embassy. Bill refused to pay for it himself and was too embarrassed to ask the Embassy for the money. Somehow Nassir ended up footing the bill. The meal (there were about thirty guests) cost 4,000ksh. Bill offered to soften the blow with a donation of 300ksh. Nassir turned it down.

*

Hassan (junior) turns up with a bottle of Ribena as an apology, I assume, for his general hopelessness about bicycles and lesson attendance. But the bicycle is still broken. I have taken it to the menders three times but each time it comes back worse. Mr and Mrs Sweet (who will be leaving Isiolo any minute) have now sold it to Kabede. But of course I can't hand it over in its present state. I am going up to Nairobi this weekend to visit Miles. I will have to take the bloody bicycle with me.

*

Kabede has given me a typed-out biography of each of his children which I am to take home to Britain with me. He is very serious about this sponsorship. He shows me their bank statements which is very stupid of him, because I now see that each of his children has an account which is overflowing with money. They've got more money in their accounts than I've ever had in mine.

So it's a little embarrassing. There are lots of people here in need of some sort of sponsorship, but it appears that Kabede's children are not among them.

*

I go to a new cafe, a very, very humble cafe (it does good mandazi), sit beside a street boy who as I walk in is shouting at the waiter to bring him tea. I am served immediately and the street boy is left shouting.

I am tired of my special privileges. I long to be sneered at in expensive shops again. I long to be kept waiting, to be left at the back of the queue.

*

I bump into a mzungu tourist who's just come from up North on his motorbike. He tells me he met a party of three girls who'd spent a week in Isiolo. They'd told him what a friendly town it was, and so he has decided to hang around for a couple of days.

The three girls, he says, had been planning to spend a few more days in Isiolo on the way back to Nairobi, but one of them couldn't quite face it. There was someone there she didn't want to bump into.

Poor Hassan. Her name was Lucy.

*

Wanjella has forgotten about the computer. Now he wants to go to university in England. I have sent for some information from UCCA, because lots of people here want to do the same thing. I tell him I will get the leaflet back from one of the teachers, make sure he sees it before I go home.

The following day he walks into my class, says he's going on safari and wants the leaflets now. The class, of which I have long ago lost all semblance of control, cackles and titters and I am very cold.

*

An urgent staff meeting is called. I walk in late. Mr make-no-mistake-I'm-a-humble-man (the Swahili teacher) is holding forth again, congratulating his headmistress on her ability to take criticism. He tells us a story about his eleven-year-old son whom he slighted somehow, some day.

'And he would not greet me. He said "I would rather cut off my hands" and he was serious. I realised how I had offended him and now it is me who calls him father!'

Some of the teachers fall asleep. Others read. He talks.

It appears that the rumblings of discontent are gathering strength. Students are threatening a strike. Mrs Tacho has been accused of favouring the Moslems. I have no idea whether or not it is true.

A school was burnt down by rioting students in another part of Kenya last week. These strikes seem to be fairly

183

common.

*

Spend the weekend driving Mr Sweet's wretched bicycle around Nairobi. We fail to find a mender. I take the bike, still broken, back to Isiolo. I will pay half the price of the bike, much more than it would cost to get it mended, if I could only get my act together and Kabede, if he accepts the deal, can mend the bicycle himself. It needs an inner tube.

*

Mr Job says it is disgraceful to drink tea at seven o'clock, but he refuses to explain to me why. He has been hassling Bill to help him with the papers he needs to set up this export business and Bill has continually refused, though I think it's supposed to be part of his job, to do anything about it.

*

My lodge still has no water. It seems to have run out of electricity since I returned from Nairobi, too. Bernard laughs when I ask him if either will ever return.

*

The science teacher draws me aside, asks if my parents would be willing to pay for him to go to university.

*

The Professor asks me to pay for his wife to come from Lodwar for the weekend. I ask how much it will cost. He hesitates, says – well, how much have you got?

*

Peter and Ali (of the one arm, marriage ceremony, stealing from Mr Sweet) have taken the Danish volunteer's house-keys and made off with 8,000ksh and two watches. They are nowhere to be seen. Japan, because he is known to be a friend of Ali's, has been put in prison. Hassan, because he is known to be a friend of Japan's, has had to spend the day at the police station.

Hassan denies all knowledge of Japan or Ali to the police, says he never was their friend, says he will never go near the Danish volunteer again.

*

'I realised,' says the Professor, 'that things were difficult for you when you said you would have to go home and look for a job . . .'

But he needs some more money.

*

I ask my class (they have exams coming up) whether they managed to find time to look at their grammar and they all say no.

Without even a hint of remorse. Just no. They are all laughing. So I ask them why not.

The boys' school has gone on strike. They want porridge for breakfast and tea at four instead of ten. Forms

1 to 3 have been sent home. The form 4s escaped their compound last night and spent five hours chasing the girls around theirs before the police could get them back under control.

A couple of policemen with rifles are standing on either side of the girls' school gate. It is a reasonable enough excuse, I suppose.

*

Fauzia puts her religion aside and comes to visit me. She finds me and Hassan and Mr Job. We are smoking and chewing and my cover is finally blown.

'You have become bad,' she says and I pretend to cough, and spit my miraa into my hand, hide it under my pillow, kick my ashtray under the bed.

Still, she invites me to lunch tomorrow to celebrate Id.

*

One of the fruit-selling women – Mary, whose husband she claims is 'mastering something, I can't remember what' in England – comes to call while I am out. Bernard sends her away, tells her I have already left Isiolo and will never be coming back. But I bump into her on the street. She seems confused to see me there. She follows me back to my room.

I am unlocking my door, asking after Kelvin (her son). Bernard comes up.

'Do you know this woman?' He is quite rude.

'Of course I do.'

'You must not have everyone in your cube. Women who are out at this time (it's nine o'clock) are bad women.

They are prostitutes. They are only friends with you so they can steal things.'

Mary, who has always been friendly, who, when I first arrived here, when I was so very, very lonely, used to spend hours teaching me Swahili, who gives me fruit and will never allow me to pay for it when I pass her tree, is reasonably offended. She shouts at him and I am cold and he tiptoes away.

*

The refugees have been arrested again. Everyone is looking for Nassir.

*

Well, and it is nearly time for me to go. Hassan has disappeared. I haven't seen him for several days. The Professor comes to say goodbye, asks me for £250, which I don't have, but he seems to forgive me.

I have fallen out with the Sweets over this bicycle. Kabede, who accepted the deal I offered then went back to the Sweets saying that an inner tube would cost him 800ksh. I know he is lying because I went to the inner tube shop this morning. It costs 100ksh. I go to say goodbye to his children.

He says: 'I won't miss you, but they will.' He doesn't mention the sponsorship and neither do I.

Fauzia cooks me biscuits and buys me a pair of shoes. My students demand that I spend our final lesson taking photographs. My last two classes are a farce; total anarchy.

They say they are sad to see me go, but then students tend to say that sort of thing. I don't know that they are.

But I am sad. Sad especially, I think, to have done my job so badly.

The teachers, except for Mr Nice, who takes far too long about it, are too snoozy to muster much warmth at my departure. But I am not sad to see the back of any of them.

And I walk down the dusty school path for the last time, past Mrs Tacho's father-in-law, who has been sitting by the gates, in that grass, in the silence, for almost a fortnight now. And I pass the children who shout mzungu! and the men who shout Seesta! and the women who stare and I don't mind that I will never see them again.

The crooked watchman, Nassir, Mr Job, Issac, the Professor and Bernard come to see me off.

But the bus doesn't leave for an hour and, eventually, I am left to wait alone. Isiolo has gone back to its business.

TIM PARKS

Italian Neighbours

'This is a clever, entertaining book. And, rare, in travel literature, it is charged with a sense of purpose'
Sunday Times

'I recommend his book to all those who are fed up with accounts of roughing it agreeably in Tuscany and similar junk that scarcely scratches the surface of the real Italy'
Paul Bailey, *Daily Telegraph*

'Gradually (he) comes to accept what the locals take for granted: everybody likes the Pope, racism thrives, the barber is a faith healer, the bank manager asks what interest rate you want to pay and the devoted church-going pharmacist upholds Catholicism on a Sunday but shows commercial flair the rest of the week by selling cut-price condoms... A rich treat from start to finish'
Sunday Express

'Synthesising the experiences of a long-standing resident into a single year... *Italian Neighbours* is not about the escape of an idyll, but about a different way of living life's idiocies and hardships'
City Limits

'Tough, funny and sceptical'
Tatler

ERROL TRZEBINSKI

The Lives of Beryl Markham
Out of Africa's Hidden Seductress

Hauntingly beautiful, tough as steel, totally amoral and immensely brave, Beryl Markham inspired lust, resentment and admiration, and was chased by scandal wherever she went. Married three times, she counted Edward Prince of Wales, his brother the Duke of Gloucester and Denys Finch Hatton – immortalised by Karen Blixen in *Out of Africa* – among her lovers. Capping notoriety with fame, in 1936 Beryl Markham became the first woman to fly solo west across the Atlantic, the feat described in her bestselling memoir *West with the Night*.

'Beryl's behaviour certainly makes for a wonderful read and I cannot recommend this book too highly'
Lady Antonia Fraser, *Mail on Sunday*

'Trzebinski has provided a richly detailed and memorable account of a woman who achieved much and fascinated and outraged in equal measure across three continents'
Literary Review

'Errol Trzebinski has researched her biography with meticulous care and spun it together with impressive skill'
Elspeth Huxley, *Daily Telegraph*

'Trzebinski combines sympathetic understanding with an evocative style'
Independent

HELEN SUZMAN

In No Uncertain Terms
Memoirs

With new information taking it up to the momentous elections in April 1994, this is the story of Helen Suzman, tireless fighter against apartheid and for the rights of the marginalised and dispossessed of South Africa.

'When the history of South Africa is written, she and her colleagues will be found to have played a very large part in the struggle for human rights – and she is very entertaining as well'
Sir David Steel

'Combative and courageous, Helen Suzman's political life is on an heroic scale'
Observer

'A wonderful woman, brave, formidable, indefatigable, witty, thinking'
Financial Times

'In all the annals of parliamentarism in the English-speaking world, Helen Suzman may have been the best there has ever been'
The Times

'I believe this book should be read by all interested in South Africa'
Nelson Mandela

A Selected List of Non-Fiction Titles Available from Mandarin

While every effort is made to keep prices low, it is sometimes necessary to increase prices at short notice. Mandarin Paperbacks reserves the right to show new retail prices on covers which may differ from those previously advertised in the text or elsewhere.

The prices shown below were correct at the time of going to press.